Journey From The East

Michael Bayliss

Journey From The East

Copyright © 2014 Michael Bayliss

All rights reserved.

www.michaelbayliss.com

Cover Design: Ian Young

All rights reserved. No part of this book may be reproduced in any form or by any electronic or mechanical means, including information storage and retrieval systems, without written permission from the author, except in the case of a reviewer, who may quote brief passages embodied in critical articles or in a review.

This is a work of fiction based around the historical figures and events of Judaism and Christianity and Chinese court records. Apart from the traditional people and events mentioned in the Holy Bible and in the Chinese History books, names, characters, places, and incidents either are the product of the author's imagination or are used fictitiously, and any resemblance to actual persons, living or dead, events, or locales is entirely coincidental.

ISBN: 1497506433
ISBN-13: 978-1497506435

DEDICATION

For Paul and Kath

For Mary. Until we see you again.

CONTENTS

Acknowledgments	i
Chapter One	1
Chapter Two	7
Chapter Three	11
Chapter Four	17
Chapter Five	24
Chapter Six	32
Chapter Seven	42
Chapter Eight	48
Chapter Nine	54
Chapter Ten	58
Chapter Eleven	66
Chapter Twelve	70
Chapter Thirteen	76
Chapter Fourteen	81
Chapter Fifteen	86
Chapter Sixteen	92
About The Author	100
Pronouncing Chinese	101

ACKNOWLEDGMENTS

A lot of the acknowledgments below are for specific help that people have given me when writing this book. Others are just to say thank you to those who have encouraged me or helped me and prayed for me.

I want to thank my wife and sons for being so understanding while I wrote this book and for believing in me. I love you guys.

Thank you to my parents; Mum for your prayers and proofreding (sic); Dad, for your knowledge of God's word, your wacky jokes and your stories.
Thank you my wonderful sisters and families. Mim and Adam, Tabitha, Ophelia and Jude. Emily and Steve, Euphrates, Isaiah, Eternity and Odette.
Thank you to other family, Eddie and Anne, Karen and Bruce, Anthony and Amy and Mandy for all your love and support.
Thanks Uncle Paul, Bec and Dave, Emma, Mark and Jenny and James and Min. Thanks Aunty Bet and Gail and John. Thanks Rod. Thanks Mike Dodd.

Thank you to everyone who gave me advice regarding content and formatting. All errors are mine and many have come from me ignoring advice.
Thank you Anna Maguire and Australian Writers' Centre for good advice and practical instruction regarding the publishing process.
Thank you Professor Sir Colin Humphreys for your inspiring scholarship on the star of Bethlehem.
Thank you George Athas and Bob Mendelsohn for your advice and answers on Biblical history. Thank you Charles Dale for giving me a desk and for buying me lunch and for hitting me when I play Starcraft 2™ instead of writing.

Thanks Felix for the coffee. Thank you Ian Young for the amazing cover. Thank you Skeeve Stevens. You will always be my sugar daddy. Thank you Valerie Ling, Sunny Hong and Rev Rick Lewis for your wise counsel.

Thank you Rosalind Hecker, Paul Cheung, Chris Choi, Annie Giang, Jenny Ihn, Pamela Chen, Andrew Lampe, Jim Dale, Hannah, Olive and Art. Thanks Cameron McPherson. Thank you all for your love.

Thank you to friends and Facebook friends (laughing or groaning at my jokes and puns) who have encouraged me on this journey: Richard, Michelle and Joshua, Ben Beilharz, Libby and John Creelman, Dan Graham, Roger Fitzhardinge, David Ould, John Bartik, Matthew Lock, Rory Shiner, Spencer McDonald, Jenny Ihn, Malvina and Marc Allison, Richard Porter, Benson Lai, Kamal Weerakoon, Ruth Brigden, Kristy and Sam Freney, Ruby Lu, Stephen Ritchie, Hugh Dircks, Andrew Haigh, Ben Beilharz, Rev Ian Powell, KahLin and Mark Wormell. If I've omitted by accident or forgotten anyone I need to thank then please forgive me and thank you. This is my first time at doing this sort of thing.

CHAPTER ONE

Bing looked up at the stars and felt small. He closed his eyes. By the position of the stars he knew that it was time to sow the fields. He took a deep breath and held it. Tomorrow his children would help him with the work. He looked back at his house, where his family were sleeping.

Bing breathed out slowly. The anticipation of a good harvest gave him optimism for the future. But he couldn't get too excited. He knew he had to work hard. As he walked back to his house, under the light of the stars, he whistled.

Bing woke to shouts outside the house. He thought it was the laborers coming early. Then he was startled, maybe it was bandits coming to take his grain and his family, his wife and children. Bing's wife was famous for her beauty and their daughters took after her. The bandits probably wouldn't kidnap his youngest son, because of his twisted face and limbs, they may even kill him.

Bing's heart beat fast, like it was trying to escape from his chest. His neck felt tight like stretched animal hide. He put his sweaty hands on the side of the wall and pulled himself up. No, he could hear the shouts now. They were cries for help and he saw that all his family were sitting around the low table in the next room. The voice kept calling from outside.

"Bing help. We need you. The Emperor needs you."

Bing ran to the open window and jumped out, not needing to exit via the door. Xiao Zhou was outside.

"Bing, some men are attacking the Emperor's envoy at the marketplace."

What was the Emperor's envoy doing this far from the capital? Surely Emperor Ai was not with them. The rumors were that he was too sick to do anything. Bing knew that whatever it was would eat into planting time but it sounded exciting.

Bing called back to his wife to keep the children inside.

"I'll be back, my love," Bing said.

"I'm not worried. Pick up some chives after you're done."

It was a five minute run to the market. With Xiao Zhou lagging behind him, Bing calculated that Xiao Zhou had probably taken ten minutes to get to his house. But it didn't matter. When Bing got to the marketplace the Emperor's envoy was still there facing off against two men. There were two other men lying on the ground. They looked dead.

Bing was right about the Emperor. The Royal banner was above Emperor Ai's messenger and his servant but the Emperor was not there. The servant was breathing heavily with blood coming from two slashes, one across his chest and one across his left leg.

Bing kneeled, bowed and put his right fist into his left palm.

"Sir. Do you need my help?"

The messenger looked at his servant. The servant nodded.

"Please ... Mister ..."

"Not a Mister, just Bing. Bing Li."

"Thank you Bing."

Bing stood up. He stood calmly with his arms by his side. No fighting stance. Not yet.

"Please leave," said Bing. "Why are you attacking the Emperor's men?"

The two men didn't say anything. One of them twirled his sword in front of him. The other man pulled a metal chain tight and started swinging it above his head.

"Are you Xiongnu, Manchu or from the South?"

The men didn't say anything.

"Before I take those toys from you, tell me, why are you attacking the Emperor's men?"

The two men twirling and swinging walked towards Bing. Bing breathed in. He put his hands into his pockets. He grabbed a handful of seeds from each one, just a small handful and flicked the seeds at both men, at their eyes. The men blinked. They kept twirling and swinging but they had lost their rhythm. Bing could hear it. They were blinking, trying to get the flecks out of their eyes.

"Here, let me help you wash it out."

Bing grabbed a gourd of clear liquid from his belt. He flicked the gourd at the men and their eyes were filled with strong alcohol that had been infused with chili. The men kept blinking, still twirling and swinging, blocking out the stinging pain, but Bing knew that they were no longer a threat.

He moved quickly and was next to the man with the sword. He punched the man's chest knocking the wind out of him. The man dropped his sword. Bing did the same thing to the man with the chain. The messenger's servant quickly tied them up. They tried to resist while struggling to breathe.

"There you go," said Bing

The Emperor's messenger pointed behind Bing. The light was dawning and it revealed another ten men. Bing smiled. He picked up the sword that the man had dropped.

"Who left this lying around? Someone might get hurt."

The Emperor's messenger smiled and turned to his servant. "Fix your wounds. I think you've got some time."

Bing looked at the men. From what he could tell, they only had swords. They didn't look as confident as the two men he had fought. Except for one. One of the men stood tall and straight. Apart from him the other men were leaning back a bit, trying to look bold but wavering ever so slightly.

Bing walked forward. The confident man walked to the front of the group with the others close behind him. Bing ran towards the front man but as he got to him he jumped onto a wooden stall and launched himself over the heads of the men, spinning in the air, landing at the back of the group. He did a sweep kick and three of the men fell over. He gave them sharp jabs on their necks, enough to render them unconscious.

The men in front turned around but were clumsy. Bing kicked one of them and the man with the two behind him fell over each other into a pile. Bing jumped on top of the pile and the men in their clumsiness couldn't get their swords out of the way in time and their swords cut into each other. From the top of the pile Bing did a split kick to the heads of the next two men and they landed with a thud. The confident man stood there. Waiting.

Bing plunged his sword down hard into the ground. He held up his fingers in front of his face.

"One, two, three, four ..." he counted, starting with open hands and curling his fingers back. He mouthed the next lot of numbers silently. Five, six, seven, eight, nine ... "Ten!" Now Bing's hands were fists.

"I swear there were ten of you a second ago."

Bing ducked, spun and punched as he heard the ninth man behind him who oafishly swung his sword. The sword went over Bing's head and Bing's punch landed in the man's groin. The man landed on the ground in pain.

The last man standing smiled at Bing.

"Ok. I'm going. You're too good for me."

"You're not allowed to go," said Bing

"Try and stop me." The man turned around and started running. He was fast.

Bing shrugged. "I didn't say I'd stop you." He had seen the Emperor's messenger grab his bow and take an arrow from the sheath that was hanging from his left leg.

The messenger pulled back the string of the bow. He let his fingers go and almost instantly the runner fell to the ground.

"Fast arrow," said Bing.

"That's what they call me in the capital. You can call me Arrow."

Bing looked at the man. "I have two questions. Why are you here, and why didn't you take down those men with your arrows? I'm sure you could have."

The Messenger looked at Bing. "You."

Bing screwed up his face. "Pardon?"

"I'm here for you. And I was waiting for you to get here. Honestly, I thought I would have to use more than just one arrow to help you out."

Bing's eyebrows scrunched up. "I'm confused."

"Bing, the fame of your wife's beauty is only surpassed by the fame of your fighting skills. Emperor Ai could do with a person like you close to him in Chang'an."

"Does he have direct need of me in the capital? I thought there was peace in the land."

"Nothing is pressing at the moment, but the Han have been weakening for some time and there are signs of disturbances in the heavens."

"Sir, It is time to sow the fields and my family are here."

"I understand. You are not full Han. You are mixed with the Koreans. But you have served the Han Emperor before and proved your allegiance."

"You can call on me after the fields are done. Then I will come and join you at the capital with my family."

"I understand."

Bing felt uneasy about the way Arrow had said he understood. His lips were too tight and his eyes had narrowed. Bing bowed. He bought some chives from Mrs. Qian and went back to his family.

CHAPTER TWO

Bing's family were waiting for him. His wife had prepared the food and all the children were sitting on the floor around the table. They were waiting for him to begin eating. Bing smiled. He looked up at the sky.

"The heavens have been kind to me today. Not even a scratch. But we must eat quickly. We have a lot of work to do."

His wife smiled and nodded. They ate in pleasant silence.

When it was time to go to the field his children got ready. His youngest son Bao tried to follow. His twisted limbs kept defeating his attempts to stand. Bing put his hand on Bao's head.

"It's OK, Bao. We'll be back in the afternoon. You stay here with mother and keep her company. Protect her."

Cute little Bao smiled and giggled, although he longed to join his father and siblings in the field.

Bing planted wheat and hemp. The Han in this part of the land were not good farmers. They tried to plant rice where wheat should go. Wheat where vegetables should go. And vegetables where hemp should go. But Bing and the surrounding Korean Chinese helped the Han to cultivate the region. They didn't have much choice. Bing and his family had been told to move up North from Lelang to help with the fields.

Now they was only a week's journey from Confucius's hometown. Bing thought that the essence of Confucius's writings were true. He just never had enough time to really sit down and study them. He suspected that sometimes the leaders of the region used his words for their own purposes, but as a peasant he could not question them. Nevertheless, he would teach his children the precepts of Confucius as they walked towards the fields. Especially the ones about respecting your father.

Bing pushed the heavy cart while his children sowed the seed. He encouraged them to throw the seeds on the field but they were sometimes too enthusiastic and the seed went everywhere.

"Daddy, we want to throw the seed on the rocks, amongst the weeds. Who knows where it will grow the best?"

Bing smiled at their optimism. He didn't want to exasperate them so he kept encouraging them to throw the seed where it should go but couldn't get angry when they were distracted.

They got into a rhythm of sowing. The children chased crows away. They pulled out weeds that were creeping up. They kicked big rocks out of the way. They covered the field with seeds and when their father wasn't watching they threw seed at each other.

The sun was unrelenting so Bing made a shelter with the cart. They sat there and ate some eggs.

"I can finish the rest. You go home and help Mother get the dinner. Tell her to prepare the lamb, it is a special day."

The children ran off and Bing sat there a while longer before he pulled himself up and finished sowing the seed.

Clouds provided some cool relief as they went across

the sun. Rain was not expected but it really looked like the sky was darkening and the air was getting heavy.

"Well, that will give the seeds a bit of help to get started. Just hope they don't get flooded and washed away."

The clouds weren't too menacing yet. Bing decided to have a rest next to the cart. He felt he had earned it after the scuffle in the early morning. And he was a good father who deserved a rest. Bing closed his eyes.

Bing sniffed the air, as the smell of smoke brought him out of his sleep. "Mmm, barbecue."

His eyes opened. There was smoke rising on the horizon, from the direction of his house. He left the cart and his tools and ran towards his family. He heard Bao screaming. He heard no noise from anyone else.

He ran to the door of his house and a man stood there with a sword. The sword was red with blood, Bing's family's blood. The man was standing with his foot on Bao who was struggling to move. Around them fire was jumping from wooden beam to wooden beam.

Bing picked up his own sword and tried to pull it out of its sheath. It was rusted stuck, he had not used it for such a long time. Bing launched himself at the man. He broke the man's arm, took the man's sword and slid the blade into the man's throat.

Another man lunged at him. Bing jumped back and jumped for the sickle that he kept hanging from the ceiling. He swung it and the man in front of him was sliced down the middle. The man fell to the floor gurgling from his mouth and from the cut in his chest.

Yet another man was bending over the bodies of Bing's wife and daughters. He looked at Bing, looked towards the door and then ran for the window. He jumped out of the window.

Bing breathed. This one he wouldn't kill. He would catch him and find out where the men were from, why they had done this. He saw the man run off in the direction of the fields which led to the mountains. He wouldn't be able to hide. First Bing went to check on Bao. He picked up his fragile son, but already twisted bones were more twisted and even broken. His son was wailing, crying with fear. Bing cried with him. Bing held him and felt his little son's life leave his body. The gasping breathes were no more and Bao stared, unblinking at the roof.

Now was not the time to cry. Everything became dark around Bing. He felt like he was amongst the stars. He felt weightless except for the weight in his heart. The weight turned to pain. It came beating up into his head. He ran to the window, the man was still running. Bing ran after him. He wanted to know why. Why had these men done this?

Bing ran but couldn't feel his feet. He felt like he was riding on a cloud, floating, flying, as he sped towards the man. Bing reached the man, put his arm on his shoulder but an arrow pierced the man's neck. And then another went between his ribs. The man slumped to the floor dead. Bing turned around.

"Why? Why?" he shouted. Arrow caught up with him.

"That man was dangerous and desperate. He would have killed you. We came back when we saw the smoke. We will find out who did this and they will pay," said Arrow.

Bing slumped. He lay on the ground face first. He tasted the soil. The world was spinning around him. He felt like the ground was a ceiling and that the sky was underneath him. He grabbed the tufts of grass. He felt that if he didn't hang on he would fall off the face of the earth. He sobbed and he sobbed as the rains hit.

Bing looked up at Arrow, both of them soaked by the rain.

"Tell the Emperor I'm a free man."

CHAPTER THREE

Bing held on to the horse as he approached the capital. He wondered what the Emperor had in store for him. It felt like there was peace in the land at the moment. Just as much peace as usual, apart from the random murdering bandits. Maybe the Emperor wanted advice with farming.

As the horse rode, the beads on the drum that had been Bao's favorite, bounced and beat in time with the noise from the horse's feet and its sound made a sort of music with the bracelet that jiggled on Bing's left wrist. There was a stone on the bracelet for each of his family members to keep them in his thoughts. For his wife a bright red stone, for his eldest son a jade stone, for his eldest daughter a blue stone, for his next son a volcanic stone, for his next daughter a marble and for Bao, his youngest, a jagged rock from the stream.

He also touched the stick that he had strapped to his right leg. It was the small, twisted crutch that Bao had used to move around. Bing closed his eyes. The horse sensed this and stopped. Arrow looked back. He stopped his horse too and waited.

Bing breathed deeply while the wave of grief trembled from his heart all over his body. He cleared his throat and spat out the dust that was gathering. He looked up and saw Arrow waiting for him.

They kept riding towards the city.

The walls had been reinforced since Bing had visited the capital. More trees and shrubbery had been cleared around the city, to make it safer and definitely more imposing. The blue sky and the crimson red banners of the city accentuated each other.

There were a lot more people too. Bing looked through the main gate. The guards were watching, observing the people and maintaining control. How did they do it? People were everywhere. Bing stared at some foreigners with paler skin. There was one man so pale he looked like the sun would burn him to a flake. He was almost as pale as the royal ladies that hid behind headdresses with tassels and umbrellas, who only showed their red pouting lips on their white powdered chins.

Although the noise was overwhelming, there was order here. There were people selling things on the side of the road. Peasants, merchants, officials, beggars, children. They all knew their place. And the peasants and merchants were happy for the moment. They grumbled about the usual things, and about the corruption amongst the officials, but as long as they had a job and food then the corruption didn't worry them. Grumbling about those in power over them was just one of the ways to pass the time, and anyway they weren't perfect themselves.

Bing and Arrow rode on to another gate closer to the middle of the city. This time the guards stopped everyone. Arrow motioned for Bing to dismount as he did the same. The guard motioned for Arrow and Bing to stop. They did. As they were waiting they heard a commotion coming from the marketplace.

People were screaming and yelling. Bing and Arrow ran in the direction of the noise. There was blood on the ground and people scrambling to get away. One child was yelling *monster, monster*. The blood was smeared on the ground leading away from the market around the corner. Bing and Arrow followed the blood.

There were two men chasing a large armored animal with a horn sticking out of its nose. The armor was part of the animal's body and not man-made.

"What's that?" asked Bing.

"The Emperor's unicorn rhinoceros. The animal keeper has been trying to tame it for some time."

"Why on earth?"

Bing saw a mother with her child trying to climb the wall to get away from the rhino. The animal keeper was holding two sticks and trying to get the rhino to turn around. The keeper was wounded on his side. It was his blood that was on the ground. On the rhino's back was a saddle. Someone had been trying to ride the rhino. What were they thinking?

The lady with her child was high up the wall and climbing higher but the rhino was charging into the rocks trying to knock the wall down.

Bing ran for the rhino and yelled, "Hayah!"

The rhino looked around. It was confused. What was this man doing?

Bing crouched, the rhino rushed at him and Bing jumped out of the way as the rhino slid past him. Bing ran for the closest gate he could find, yelling at people to get out of his way.

As the rhino came close to him he jumped off the wall and somersaulted back behind the rhino.

"How do I stop this thing?"

The animal keeper caught up. "We have to tranquilize it."

"Where are the tranquilizers?" asked Arrow.

"Um ..."

"Where are they?"

"In my room."

"Where's that?"

"On the other side of the city."

Arrow rolled his eyes.

"Go! Let's get them now! Bing. Try and lead it out of the city."

Bing nodded. He ran towards the rhino and darted from side to side, dodging and jumping. The mother and her child were safe for now. Bing was relieved, though every time he ran too far away from the rhino it would get distracted and try to pick a fight with anyone or anything around it.

"Come on. Come and get me."

The rhino kept charging but then stopped. It was running past one of the street stalls that served barbecued vegetable skewers.

The lady who had been selling the skewers was hiding behind her stall. The rhino charged the stall and flipped it into the air. The rhino wasn't concerned anymore about Bing's yells and taunts. He wanted the lady who was covered in vegetables. She smelt good to him. The lady couldn't run anywhere. She spied a cleft in the wall and tried to squeeze inside.

The rhino couldn't reach her, but he was trying his best to make the hole bigger. *Bham! Bham!* He kept thudding into the wall.

Bing ran up and punched the back of the rhino. It didn't even flinch. Bing looked at the saddle.

"No!" he thought. Whoever had tried to do that was a crazy man. He kept punching the rhino but the rhino's hide was too thick. Bing decided to go for it, he jumped on the rhino's back, onto the saddle and found the reins that were thankfully still tied to a bit in the rhino's teeth. He pulled hard on the reigns and the rhino growled but stopped barging the wall.

The rhino went up on hind legs and tried swaying left and right but Bing held on. The rhino slowly pivoted. It walked down the main street. Bing couldn't believe it. He had calmed the rhino. He now had control of it.

The rhino was walking past the shopkeepers who were

peering out from their hiding places. They all came out and started cheering. Bing felt like a King. He even laughed and waved a funny little wave.

But Bing wasn't in control. The rhino was just playing with him. It spotted the open front gate and it started to run. Bing who was still holding on with only one hand and waving, held on tight as the rhino knocked down the guards in the gateway.

Arrow was on the battlements. He had found a tranquilizer arrow and had climbed up to get a good view for a shot. He saw Bing and the rhino leave the city and he knew he had to shoot fast. He aimed for the backside of the rhino. The arrow flew swiftly towards the rhino's bottom, but it didn't pierce, it ricocheted off the rhino and straight up into Bing's side.

"Ayaa!" said Arrow. He slid down the side of the wall, using his bow to slow his descent, scraping it on the wall.

Arrow landed on the ground. He saw Bing fall backwards unconscious as the sedative mingled with his blood. Sensing that Bing was no longer trying to control him, the rhino slowed. Bing slipped off his back and thudded to the ground. The rhino slowed to a stop and turned around. It stared at Bing with anger.

Arrow saw the danger. Bing was going to be ravaged by the great beast unless he could do something.

Arrow had prepared a tranquilizer tip for his crossbow too. Arrow aimed the crossbow and the bolt went through the throat of the rhino as it charged Bing. The rhino thrashed but slowed down. Two guards were riding towards it. One with a large axe brought it down on the rhino's neck as it got close to Bing. The other rider managed to rope the rhino and pull it back so as it fell it missed Bing by a hand span.

Arrow took Bing to a room where a doctor attended to him.

Arrow saw Bing's eyes open which was unexpected because the sedative was ultra powerful. Arrow smiled at him. "You look like a man who doesn't care about your own life."

"Did everyone get away safely? The mother and child? The vegetable lady?"

"Yes. All safe. Now you need some sleep."

"No. I'm fine, I want to get up." Bing's eyes closed and he slept for two days.

CHAPTER FOUR

"The Emperor will see you when you are ready."

Bing frowned. He hadn't prepared himself to see the Emperor so early and after the rhino incident he wasn't sure what to expect.

"Is everything OK?" asked Bing

Bing followed Arrow into a courtyard. Here there were trees and a stream. The walls were high and blocked out the city, sounds and all.

"It's so quiet." Bing said.

"Yes. This place is for healing. Body and heart."

A surge of grief gripped Bing.

"Wait here while I see how long we have."

Arrow walked through a small doorway and Bing sat down on a bench.

There was a bird singing. Bing hadn't noticed it before. Had it just started? He could have sworn that there was total silence a moment ago. There wasn't just one bird singing, he could hear at least ten birds, maybe more. And there was the soft sound of a frog from the stream. Had these sounds been there all along?

Bing went to the water. There was a scoop for drinking. He drank some of the water and felt it cool his body. He looked around and when he was sure no one was watching he poured some over his head. He sat down on the bench again. He listened. He was back in the fields. Back with his family. His wife's arms around him and her breath on his neck.

Then he remembered his youngest son once knocking the food off the table by accident. How he had got angry despite himself and yelled, then immediately felt regret. Why did he have this thought now? Why out of all the good memories of his family would he think about this bad memory? He felt guilty.

Bing breathed in sharply, all the different fragrances from the flowers around him rushed into his nose, he felt dizzy. The feelings of his family faded. He was surrounded by darkness again. He was alone.

"Bing."

A woman's voice called to him.

"Bing."

For a moment Bing thought it was his wife. Then he remembered where he was.

"Yes," Bing said.

"I am here to get you ready to see the Emperor. You can't see him dressed like that."

Bing was wearing his best clothes. Of course, they weren't good enough for the royal court. Bing wondered why they had sent a young woman to help him prepare. As he followed her he noticed two other ladies walking alongside him.

"Bing, Arrow said you may need some assistance preparing."

Bing shook his head. "Just show me where my clothes are. I can dress myself thanks."

Bing didn't know why Arrow had sent these three women. They looked at him attentively. Bing thought it better to keep his distance. He felt like it was some sort of test.

The woman said again, "No, really. Arrow said we are

yours. How can we help you?"

Bing didn't want to sound rude but it came out gruffly. "Just show me my clothes."

The women giggled. They pointed to the door. Bing went in and dressed himself.

The Emperor's court was just as Bing had seen in paintings. The Emperor sitting in the middle of a large hall. Guards and statues of guards standing to attention. But there were a lot more people standing near the Emperor than Bing expected. He didn't look so aloof.

Arrow looked at Bing and could tell he was nervous.

"Bing. It's ok, he's just a man. You need to calm down."

"What do I do?"

"Just answer him when he asks you something, or nod when he says something to you. Oh, and bow when I bow."

Arrow and Bing waited as other people were introduced to the Emperor. There were officials advising the Emperor on civil affairs; merchant princes requesting thoroughfare through China; poets and scholars dedicating their work to the Emperor. The Emperor looked bored.

Arrow and Bing were beckoned towards the Emperor. The Emperor was trying to suppress a cough. He coughed into his sleeve. He shook his sleeve out. Phlegm had got stuck in the hem. A servant brought the Emperor a cup. He drank from the cup and patted his stomach. He coughed again.

Arrow bowed in front of the Emperor at the edge of the rug. Bing did the same. Arrow stood up. Bing did the same.

"Thank you for coming," said the Emperor. He raised his cup. It was the rhinoceros's horn.

"Thank you. I had been wanting his horn for sometime but couldn't bring myself to kill him. He was so cute."

Bing expected something more grand, something more

elaborate. He smiled and nodded.

"I'm sorry to hear about your family."

Bing nodded again, without smiling. The Emperor approached Bing. Arrow had never seen something like this. Usually the Emperor would stay seated and never approach a guest. The Emperor examined Bing's body. He gripped Bing's biceps.

"Very strong," said the Emperor. "Such intense eyes." The Emperor put his hand on Bing's chest. "Good heart."

Bing felt uneasy as the Emperor's hand lingered on his chest, he tried to breathe calmly but could feel his muscles tense. The Emperor smiled a soft smile then went back to his seat and sat down. The Emperor looked around at those standing near him.

"I was planning to have you stay with us at the palace. A strong man like you can be very helpful."

The advisor standing closest to the King smiled.

"Some people think I am weak and they think that weak Kings don't get assassinated ... only strong Kings. Well. I'll show everyone that I'm strong." The King coughed as he said those words and needed someone to pat him on the back.

The Emperor regained his composure and looked at Bing.

"I need you for something more than just guarding the palace. It looks like there is something rising on the horizon. I'll bring in my advisor to tell you."

An old man walked to the front. He didn't smile. He didn't have much facial expression at all. Except one eye was looking at Bing and the other eye was doing its own thing. It was looking up and darting here and there, as if it was fascinated by the patterns on the roof.

"We need you to escort our astronomer's apprentice to find the chief astronomer Liu Xiang. He has been missing for some months now. You are to go and assist him with whatever he needs. He was talking about making an alliance with a kingdom in the West or something like that."

Bing didn't quite understand what the man meant.

"There is a saying, "Make friends with those far away and pester those who are close." This I believe is what the astronomer had in mind and this is why you must find him and help him."

"I disagree. It is also true that the rabbit does not eat the grass around its own burrow." The interrupter's voice was loud and startled everyone including the Emperor.

The first advisor turned around.

"What does that even mean? Look chancellor, just shut up! We've already talked about this. The Emperor has already stamped his seal on the official command."

The chancellor kept speaking. "We just need Liu Xiang brought home or silenced. If we send someone to the West, then the nomads will definitely think we are being aggressive and will step up their attacks. We are at our most vulnerable ..."

"That's exactly why we need to go and form an alliance now. We are at our weakest. We need help."

"We have people working on an alliance with Bactria as well as Parthia. Why don't we keep negotiating with them for an alliance?"

"All of the people you have mentioned are squabbling amongst themselves. How do we know whom to choose?"

"We don't know anything about those with whom Liu Xiang is seeking an alliance. His head is in the clouds. Talking about this star and that constellation and the scrolls and ..."

While the advisors were arguing, Bing looked around the room using just his eyes, without moving his head.

Behind the Emperor was a lady. The Emperor's mother perhaps. She didn't look sick. She looked in control. It was never the person who was giving the orders that was in control but the person behind them. Another younger lady, the Emperor's wife, was behind him. Her eyes were veiled, but Bing could tell from her posture that she was staring at the ground.

Another man stood near the Emperor. He looked carefully groomed and held two scrolls under his arm. He had celestial signs stitched into his clothes. And there was an embroidered gold star on his hat, which Bing thought made him look rather comical.

"Silence," said the Emperor. "The orders have been given and we have listened to you both argue long enough. Bing, you will prepare for your journey and then leave with the astronomer's assistant."

Arrow bowed and Bing imitated him. The man with the scrolls did likewise and the three left the room. Outside the royal chamber Arrow nodded at the man with the scrolls.

"Bing this is the astronomer's apprentice. You can call him Star. You will go with him."

"Honored to meet you," said Star and smiled. Bing thought his eyebrows moved strangely and realized it was because they were not real but painted on.

Arrow put his arm on Bing's shoulders. "Let's get you ready for your journey."

Bing was putting on his travel clothes and packing away his good silks when he heard a shout from down the hallway. Arrow had left moments before to prepare the horses.

Bing ran to have a look. He saw a figure dressed in black attacking Star. Star was stabbed a number of times and then the attacker ran to the window and disappeared.

Star was holding the scrolls that he had been holding earlier, his blood was dripping onto them.

"Don't worry about me. Look after the writings. Take them to Liu Xiang."

Arrow ran into the room and saw Bing holding Star.
"Too late! He jumped out the window," said Star.
Arrow ran to the window.
"Impossible." Arrow looked around.

Bing lay Star on the ground and went to look out the window too. It was a sheer wall too high from the ground for anyone to be able to jump out and survive and too high to the roof to be able to climb.

"He's still in the palace."

Arrow ran out and sounded the alarm. The whole palace was locked down. The guards searched high and low but no one was found. The Emperor called for Arrow and Bing again.

"You two must leave immediately," said the Emperor.

"But I'm to be married in a month ..." said Arrow.

"That can wait," said the Emperor. "Go now!"

Arrow nodded and grabbed Bing, dragging him to the stable. "We are to ride now. First Gansu, then Dunhuang, and then Jiaohe. That's where Liu Xiang was last sighted." Arrow shook his head. "I don't think it's a good idea though. We should find whoever killed his assistant first."

"But the Emperor thinks it's a good idea?"

"The Emperor doesn't know what he thinks."

"Couldn't you get in trouble for saying that?"

"Look. It's at least two weeks ride to Jiaohe. And then what? We just ask around? Those cities are full of nomads and who knows who else."

"But we have to go?"

"Yes. We have no choice. As they say, "When the Emperor farts, his servants must sing an Opera."

CHAPTER FIVE

The ride to Gansu was uneventful. Bing tried not to think about his family. He just stared ahead. The sameness of the landscape comforted him. Giant rocks and trees passed by. Mountains on either side herded Bing and Arrow like sheep along the road.

At Gansu no one knew any recent news about Liu Xiang. Bing heard the usual grumbling about the leaders of the country but nothing like treason. They picked up two new horses from the Royal stables.

Then onto Dunhuang. They rode between snow covered mountains whose names Bing did not know. Arrow was in no mood to provide a commentary. They rode in silence. Bing pulled his fur coat up and his fur cap down to protect himself from the chilly wind. The long fortified wall that snaked beside them to the North did not provide any shelter from the weather.

As they entered desert terrain Bing was worried. They rode for great stretches where there was only sand and rock. Bing could feel sand covering him, getting into his clothes, in his hair, in his eyes. Then after a few days of riding when Bing was really starting to worry, Arrow shouted, "Have you ever seen an oasis?"

Bing looked up ahead. He thought that Arrow was playing a trick on him and they were just looking at a mirage. But no, there was a beautiful crescent lake, sky blue with a small wooden village draped around it.

Arrow was surprised when they rode up to the hotel and there was no room.

"Oh, royal messenger?" they said. "Yep, still no room."

If the weather had been worse, Arrow would have complained more but there were so many foreigners around and he didn't want to create a scene.

"We'll stay in a temple."

Arrow and Bing went to the second temple along the street and asked for a room. They were shown the way by a Taoist monk.

"Why not stay in the Buddhist temple instead?" asked Bing. "It's bigger isn't it?"

"Yeah, It's bigger," said Arrow. "The food's better here.

Arrow and Bing were shown a room. Bing lay down on the cushions.

"You stay here and rest. You're not as used to all this riding as I am."

"Yeah. My legs are killing me."

"Just wait. We'll be switching to camels soon."

Bing didn't know if that was a good thing or a bad thing. He lay back and fell into a deep sleep almost straight away. But he was aware that he was asleep. His body wanted to remember his family, remember his wife. His head hurt, his heart ached.

Arrow was sitting, watching Bing.

"Was I asleep long?"

"Don't worry about it."

"What's the plan?"

"Well. Liu Xiang did pass through here. He was charting the sky but then he journeyed further West. So we ride on to Jiaohe. See if Liu Xiang is there. We have to be careful from now on as we'll be taking the summer route and the roads are not busy. More chance of bandits."

"When do we leave?"

"Now."

"But you haven't rested."

"You were asleep for a long time. I got some rest."

Bing pulled on his leather boots. "I'll need to get new soles for these soon. I've never travelled this far, this fast before."

"There will be someone in Kashi if we need to travel that far. They have everything there."

Arrow and Bing rode off from the Oasis. There was a strong breeze. At times it helped them, and at times it did all it could to stop them from travelling further.

They managed to get past most of the sand and dunes and the travelling became easier. As they saw an intense red mountain range in the distance Arrow yelled back at Bing, "Jiaohe is a few hours past those mountains."

As they neared the mountains, it looked like the rocks were on fire.

"Don't worry, it's just the sun reflecting off the rocky hills ... It's not actually ..."

Fire erupted from underneath Arrow. He only just managed to stay on his horse.

"That's never happened before. Be careful."

"Watch out," said Bing.

Another hole opened up next to Arrow and a fire ball blasted up into the air. Arrow looked at the ground to see if there was any indication of a path they could follow. The ground felt shaky.

"Quick, to the high ground."

They rode away from the fire to the rocky hills. Arrow saw riders on the mountains. They looked like Xiongnu from what Arrow could tell. Their bows confirmed his suspicion. Arrow saw they had their bows drawn and pointed at them. Behind Bing and Arrow were the fire pits, in front of them up the hill were the archers.

Arrow took out his bow.

"What are you doing?" Bing looked at Arrow. He was good with the bow but there were many Xiongnu. Bing didn't like their chances. "We need help."

"Thanks. Who's going to help us."

"I don't know."

"Hey!" A lady's voice called out. It was difficult to hear with the sound of the ground erupting behind them.

"There." Bing pointed. A lady was calling to them from a cave in the rock. She was only a short distance in front of them but near the archers.

"She's our only hope," said Arrow. "Quick!"

They rode towards the cave. As they got close the Xiongnu fired on them. A volley of arrows was above them, coming down like deadly rain.

"This is going to hurt," said Bing as they made for the cave. As the arrows came down the lady stepped out of the cave and put her hands together and then thrust them at the arrows. The arrows were blown to the side, landing just beyond Bing and Arrow. No one was injured. It was like a whirlwind had come out of the lady's arms, saving them from danger.

"Good," said Bing.

"Quick. There's only enough room for you and your horses in here. You'll have to squeeze."

Inside, the cave was set up like a comfortable home, but it was hot.

"Ha. That'll scare them," said the lady. "Those Xiongnu will think I've got some superpowers or something."

Arrow and Bing were calming their horses and looked at the woman.

"How did you do that?" asked Arrow.

"I didn't. Just made it look like I did."

"What?"

"I don't want to give away too many of my secrets.

27

Let's just say I've got good timing."

Bing sat down.

"Will they follow us?"

"No. It's too steep from where they are. And anyway, my son will close up the entrance you came in. We'll leave from another way."

A younger lady brought the two men water. They were thirsty, they drank.

"Have some salted pork. It will help you drink more water, otherwise you'll pee it all out."

The men looked at each other, sat down and chewed the pieces of dried pork. They drank more water.

"Why did you help us?" asked Arrow.

"Come and meet my husband. My daughter will look after your horses. And on that, you had better start thinking about changing to camels soon. Much more practical on sand."

Bing was trying to work out what had happened. The ground had attacked them, forcing them up to the mountain. The Xiongnu were waiting there ready to skewer them with arrows. But now they were safe, although very hot, in this nice family's home.

They followed the lady expecting to walk further into a cramped cave, but the tunnel opened up into a great hall. And there were more people. There were older people writing on scrolls, others were teaching the children. There were men and women reciting poetry. There were boys and girls playing, sometimes fighting.

At a table sat a man with a long white beard. He beckoned to the two newcomers.

"I see my wife brought you safely inside."

"They were almost punctured, but the mountain gusts were as frequent and strong as always. I put on a good show." The lady danced around, replaying her earlier moves. "Maybe I should use a fan or something next time. Add to the dramatic effect."

The man smiled. "You have to be careful. One day

people will see through your powers."

"Thank you for your help, but we ..." started Arrow.

"You are looking for Liu Xiang. I know," said the old man.

"You know where he is?"

"He's in Kashi, being held prisoner by the Xiongnu and the foreigners. Even the Han General knows he is in the prison but hasn't done anything about it."

Arrow looked at Bing.

"We will rescue him."

"Of course you will. But you will need help. The Han and the Xiongnu have a little deal going on in that city and they do not want Liu Xiang and the others to make an alliance with any western forces."

"I will make sure the Emperor knows that the Han forces are collaborating with the Xiongnu."

"Of course he already knows. He doesn't care."

Arrow looked offended and confused.

The old man continued. "I'll give you some men ... and women ... to help you rescue your astronomer."

"When will the ground calm down?"

"Don't worry. We'll take you all the way to Jiaohe. From there you can plan your rescue from Kashi which is about six days away."

"A week? That's too long."

"All we can do to ensure no one sees you. We've got people in Kashi looking out for Liu Xiang and the others. They aren't worried."

Arrow and Bing were guided, sometimes through tunnels, sometimes through open air ditches to Jiaohe. Jiaohe was an entire city carved out of rock. The guide showed Arrow and Bing to one of the houses carved into the rocky hillside. "People who can help you are in here. I'll stand guard."

These rock houses were a lot cooler than the ones at Fire Mountain. People had cut holes through the walls that sucked in the cooler air and pushed out the hot air. Arrow and Bing entered through the doorway.

Sitting in front of them were men and women, some with very white skin, some with dark skin, some with dark hair but a few with yellow hair. They were all foreigners.

"Oh, I think we've got the wrong house," said Arrow.

"No," said one man in Chinese. "We have been waiting for you. To help you rescue Liu Xiang. He told us to wait for you."

"How did he know that we would come?"

"Men like him know lots of things."

"I'm Arrow and this is Bing."

"I'm Jacob. I'm the leader of this mixed group." Jacob was overweight but he looked strong and fit. He had dark skin with short black hair. He had green eyes. Bing kept staring at them.

"Haven't seen many non-Chinese have you?" said Jacob in Greek and smiled. "We're going to have lots of fun together." Bing couldn't understand a word he said.

"How do you know Liu Xiang?" asked Arrow.

"We are his trading partners," said Jacob. He was going to help open trade with China. Now it looks like he has got himself into some sort of trouble."

Arrow and Bing worked with Jacob on a plan and afterwards they had some food before resting. Jacob gave them bread dipped in olive oil with brown vinegar and some fish. The fish was fried to a crisp and covered in chili paste. They had beer to wash everything down. They slept well.

They woke up early and left Jiaohe, riding on camels with the desert on the South and the Mountains on the north. They didn't have to worry about bandits because the roads were full of travelers however they still kept an eye out for the Xiongnu riders.

At night, strange sounds came from the dessert. Arrow said it was the souls of people who had entered and never left and who would be tormented for eternity. Bing thought the sound was actually rather pleasant and that Arrow was just being dramatic.

CHAPTER SIX

Kashi was the most mixed up city Bing had seen. There were people from all over the world. They all had their little areas, speaking their own languages. If there was any tension amongst the people, Bing couldn't sense it. There was a strong Xiongnu presence at Kashi although the Han were still in control.

"There are so many foreigners here," said Bing to no one in particular. He hadn't seen anyone with orange hair before. He wondered if the orange hair was burning to touch. He didn't bring himself to ask or try to find out.

Jacob and the others who were to help in the rescue of Liu Xiang entered the city by a secret path. Bing and Arrow entered through the front gates.

At the gates, the travelers were welcomed by the Han guards and they were taken to the Governor who was also the army General.

"I know nothing of Liu Xiang," said the Han General. "He must have been captured or killed on the road."

Arrow said nothing. He knew that they were holding Liu Xiang.

The travelers were treated to a feast. They told the General that they planned to return to the capital the next day. Arrow asked if he could have a tour of the city. The General looked nervous but he sent him off with two guides. When Arrow returned he went to Bing.

"I think I know where Liu Xiang is. The guides wouldn't take me to the Western wall and tower."

Arrow and Bing went and found Jacob and his crew. Jacob nodded. "The dungeons are near the Western wall."

They waited until dusk and approached the dungeon building. They hid behind nearby trees. As the sun fell, other people started gathering and hiding in and around the nearby trees and buildings. One man almost stepped on Arrow's feet.

"What are you doing?" asked Arrow.

"What are you doing?" asked the man in a strange accent. Arrow recognized him as one of the travelers that he had seen on the road a few days back.

"Are you Xiongnu?"

"No," said the man in his flatter and more staccato style of Chinese. "I'm from the land of Wa."

"You've travelled a long way."

"From the very place where the Sun begins his day. One of our astronomers travelled here and we lost track of him. Recently we have found that he is being held here."

"What was he doing?"

"I don't know exactly. He had his head in the stars."

"I think we're here for the same reason."

"You've come to rescue our astronomer too?"

Arrow looked at the man.

"Sorry. You've come to rescue someone else."

Next to the man were two women in black clothes. Arrow looked at them.

"They are my bodyguards. Extremely deadly."

Arrow nodded. More people were collecting in the shadows. Arrow looked around and liked what he was seeing. They didn't have to do things as carefully as they had planned. The people in the shadows outnumbered the guards on duty.

Arrow stood up and in a soft but commanding voice said. "Let's storm the dungeon, together. Do not kill the guards. Harm, but do not kill."

People poured out of the shadows and overpowered the guards. The guards had no real interest in fighting back. They surrendered extremely quickly when they saw how many people they were up against. Liu Xiang and others were waiting patiently. When the rescue was completed Liu Xiang assumed control and led the travelers and all the prisoners with him to a building with a tall tower.

"Quick. Everyone inside," said Liu Xiang. He stood tall, his white hair and beard shining in the moonlight.

A great crowd gathered in the large room. There was Liu Xiang with his rescuers Bing and Arrow. An astronomer from Wa and his three rescuers. Amongst the others, Bing even saw another group from his home peninsula. He wasn't in a mood to talk to them. They reminded him of his family.

"You rescued us just in time," said Liu Xiang. "For the last two years, in many different ways, the heavens have been telling us to prepare for the birth of a mighty King. Now we are waiting for the final sign, any day a star will rise in the East to guide us. It will rise above us as we travel and take us to this new King. All of you have come from different countries to honor this King and to make an alliance with his people."

Some of the travelers whispered in excitement, some in disbelief.

"All of us coming together foreshadows the peace that this King will bring."

The advisor from Wa said. "Some people don't want peace. They like the power that war and division brings."

As he was speaking, five men ran up into the room from the tower. They looked like they were Xiongnu. Arrow drew his bow and Bing drew his sword and ran towards the men.

"Stop," said Liu Xiang. "Not all Xiongnu are bad. These are men I met before I was put in prison. They want to be part of our journey. They hope for peace too."

Bing looked around at the mix of people. He liked this idea of peace, of working together. He hadn't realized this was what the journey was all about. Was this what the Emperor had in mind when he sent them off? To search for peace? Bing had known peace once, life on the farm. He wished his family were here with him now.

A lady wearing an orange robe turned to the people and said, "For some of you it feels like you have already been on a long journey. But our real journey starts now. Together we will head towards the West to pay our tributes as priests and representatives of our Kings and Emperors. This majestic and powerful King will in time help us to band together and give us power over anyone who opposes Peace."

Everyone cheered. Bing felt uneasy about the talk of having power over those who would oppose Peace. It seemed like using peace as an excuse for war. But he wasn't a philosopher and he hadn't thought enough about it. He would have to ask Liu Xiang more about it if he got the chance.

"We will ready ourselves for our journey. We are working out the best route to get us over the Pamir mountains," said Liu Xiang.

The local hosts who were looking after the group told the travelers of a short cut through the mountains but said that it was dangerous. If there was a blizzard then the Ice Dragon would be invoked. They also told the travelers to use mules instead of camels.

Liu Xiang held up a bronze water bowl.

"Many of you have seen already that there are people trying to stop us. Even the land is rising up to hinder us. So be righteous and cleanse yourselves. Be on guard against your own thoughts and doubts."

The travelers went away to pray and to wash. There were Taoists, Buddhists and other assorted religions represented in the group but they all had a sense of needing to purify themselves. Bing noticed a lady amongst the crowd who wasn't paying attention. She was trying to blend in. Her clothes looked like that of a man, but this did not detract from her beauty. Some guards were let in through the front door. The Han General was with them.

"You're Liu Xiang. Why didn't you tell us? We were told that you were a dangerous criminal."

"You knew who I was. To save you from losing face I'm going to pretend you didn't know."

The General looked at Liu Xiang, uncertain of what to say.

"Ah. So, I've had a talk to the Xiongnu and the other guards and you are free to go. But, now, some of the prisoners who were rescued were actually real prisoners. We need to take them back."

The General looked across at the woman hiding in the crowd. Liu Xiang started to say that there were no real prisoners with them. As he spoke, the lady, frightened, ran for the stairs and up the tower.

"Stop her!" yelled the guard as three other guards ran up the stairs. Four more ran out the front door to try and stop her. Bing ran out the front door to see what would happen. The lady kept running up the tower and then jumped across to the next building. Bing could not tell if she was Chinese or a foreigner. Bing wanted to help her, he didn't know why. Was it because she was a woman, was it because she was beautiful? He felt silly and confused.

Liu Xiang turned to Arrow.

"Go and help that lady. She'll be very useful on our journey. She's fluent in many tongues."

Arrow ran out of the house and saw that Bing was doing what he could to help. He had knocked out three guards already. Two guards had caught up with the woman and Arrow aimed his bow over their heads. He knocked a flower pot off the wall and it landed on the first guard who fell over and landed on the second guard. Bing ran towards where the woman had landed after jumping off the roof and stood between her and two more guards.

Bing didn't need to use any effort. He punched both guards and sent them back into the wall.

"Quick, come with me," the woman said to Bing.

"I'll tell Liu Xiang you are safe," said Arrow.

Bing and the woman nodded. They ran off into the shadows with more guards coming to look for them.

"I tried to stop them," Arrow said to the guards. "They escaped."

Arrow went back to Liu Xiang where the Han General was arguing with him.

"Look. That lady's a criminal. You have to bring her back to me if you find her."

"She's not a criminal," said Liu Xiang.

The General huffed and walked off. "We will find her."

Arrow walked up to Liu Xiang.

"They are safe?" asked Liu Xiang.

"Yes. They will join you when it is safe before you leave."

"What's the man's name?"

"Bing. Bing Li."

"I like Bing Li. He appears to be a righteous man. Now what's this about us leaving? You're coming with us."

"No. I have to get back to the capital."

"Arrow. Under orders of the Emperor you are coming with us."

"No."

"Didn't the Emperor's mother tell you to find me and make sure I never came back?"

Arrow looked startled.

"What?"

"I know things Arrow. I know the Emperor's mother isn't impressed with her son. That she wants me and his other advisors out of the picture."

"I'm sorry."

"No problem. I quite like how you would disobey her on this. Or do you just think that the journey is too dangerous and you are confident we wouldn't return."

Arrow looked out the window.

"I know you want to do the right thing Arrow. You don't like doing the Emperor's mother's dirty work. The Emperor's command still stands and it is stronger than his mother's. You must accompany us on our journey. I need you and Bing."

"No. I'm returning to the capital."

Carissa walked in the direction of the dungeon. She wasn't listening to Bing's pleas to stop.

"You can't go back to the dungeon. They'll capture you," said Bing.

"You'll protect me. I saw you just then," said Carissa.

"No. It will be a lot more difficult."

"I'm getting my stuff."

"Ok. I'll go. You just tell me what to get."

Carissa stopped and looked at Bing. "Danke."

"What does that mean?"

"Thank you ... in another language."

They made their way back to the dungeons, right next door to the Xiongnu headquarters.

"I don't get why they are allowed such a big presence here."

"They've got powerful friends. The Han give them some concessions and they don't cause too much trouble. And anyway, it's not just the Xiongnu ... I mean they aren't just one people, they are a group of nomads who work together."

"Ok, what am I looking for?"

"My jacket and my shoes."

"What? You want me to risk my life for some clothes? I can buy you new ones at the market."

"Look. They aren't just any clothes. The jacket has my scrolls in it and some other things."

"Oh, I see. And the shoes?"

"They're red. My favorite."

Bing rolled his eyes.

He climbed up onto the roof of the dungeon and edged across to the side. There were guards below him sitting around a fire. He threw a piece of rock into the fire which at first didn't make a noise but then it made a *pop* and the guards looked into the fire. Then he flicked another stone so it made a noise at the far fence and the guards with blurry eyes looked away into the darkness. Bing let himself down into the room. He rolled down behind some chests and then walked behind two guards who were having an argument about who was fatter.

Most of the guards didn't seem to care about their job too much. And as there was only a handful of prisoners left after today's raid, everything was quiet. Bing found Carissa's jacket and shoes. He went to leave but overheard the guards talking.

"Pigeon arrived from the capital. The Emperor's mother wants Arrow killed, as well as the others."

"After today, I want him killed as well. He's going to ruin everything we've worked out between the Han and the Xiongnu."

Bing exited the dungeon. No one saw him.

"Here." He gave Carissa's things to her. She checked her pockets to make sure everything was there.

Bing in a quiet voice said, "We're in trouble. Arrow especially."

"Who's Arrow?"

"Kind of my boss."

"The one with the arrows? He's handsome."

Bing wondered why she had told him that.

"I've got to tell everyone that we need to leave now," said Bing.

Arrow was packing his horse.

"What are you doing?" asked Bing.

"Your job is to escort Liu Xiang on the foolish journey, chasing the stars. I'm going back to the capital."

"You're in danger."

"We're always in danger. That's life."

"Ai's mother has ordered your death, along with all of us."

Arrow looked at Bing. "Who told you that?"

Bing told Arrow and Arrow leant on his horse.

"I wonder if the Emperor knows."

"So you will come with us on our journey?"

"No. I'm going to go back and kill the Emperor's mother myself."

"Even though you are good, you're not that good," said Bing.

Carissa walked up to the two men.

"So you're the lady with the talented tongue," said Arrow.

"Excuse me?"

"Er ... I mean, Liu Xiang said you were good at languages."

"And you must be Arrow."

Arrow and Carissa looked at each other. Bing stood uncomfortably next to them. They kept staring at each other.

"So? What's happening?" asked Bing.

"Ah ... we leave for the West tomorrow," Arrow said.

"You're coming now?"

"Yeah. I was always coming," Arrow said.

"What about your wife?" asked Bing.

"Wife?" asked Carissa and cleared her throat.

"Was only going to meet her on the wedding day. She won't be too sad. Anyway ... I'm a marked man."

Jacob walked up and smiled at Arrow. "Looks like Cupid has shot himself."

Arrow looked away.

"I'll be joining you. Me and my servants," said Jacob. "I don't believe in the star or the King, but business opportunities like this don't come along every day. Look at all these people from different parts of the world working together."

"We have to leave now. Let's go and get everyone," said Bing.

Arrow looked at Carissa in the moonlight saddling the mules.

"What do you think she is?" asked Bing in a whisper.

"She's beautiful," said Arrow.

"No. What do you think she is? Greek, Roman, Persian, Nomad?"

"Probably all of them."

"Mother's dad was from Rome and her mother was Greek. My father is half Chinese, half Indian," said Carissa not looking at them.

Bing smiled and looked away and Arrow kept staring at her.

"I didn't know you could hear us," said Arrow.

Carissa smiled. "I've got good ears. I can read your thoughts too."

Arrow blushed. Liu Xiang walked towards the group.

"Good to see that you are joining us," Liu Xiang said to Arrow.

Liu Xiang walked with Bing.

"Arrow told me about your family."

Bing nodded.

"I'm sorry to hear about your loss. I'm glad that you are with us."

Bing felt warmth towards this old man. He looked around at all the people who had gathered. Bing wondered if they would all be able to work together to cross the mountains ahead of them. They had to make sure that they got away from the city safely but even that would not mean that they were out of danger.

CHAPTER SEVEN

The travelers left as soon as they could, sneaking out of the city. They were making good ground when the Xiongnu and the Han Guards started pursuing. They were chased to the bottom of the mountains and as they arrived mist started swirling around them. The Xiongnu and Guards stopped at the base of the mountains.

"So you're going the easy way. If you go up there the Ice Dragon will devour you. If you try and come back we will kill you," said the Xiongnu chief.

Everyone looked to Liu Xiang for leadership.

"We'll keep going through the mountains."

"Dragons don't exist," said Arrow to Carissa.

"How can you say that?" asked Carissa.

"I've been all over China and beyond. I've never seen one," said Arrow.

"That doesn't mean they don't exist. The stories say that the Ice Dragon is invisible."

Arrow laughed.

As they made their way into the mountain the mist and fog grew thicker. They trudged forward. Arrow felt confident that they would all be fine. The terrain was cumbersome, jagged rocks and prickly shrubs. They decided to stop for the night.

Carissa and Liu Xiang were deep in discussion. Arrow sat with Bing and taught him how to play Wei Qi. The astronomer from Wa watched. He said that he called the game Go. Arrow had a special metallic board with grids on it and white and black magnetic stones. This magnetic board allowed him to pack the Wei Qi into his luggage and so pause the game when needed because most games took about four to eight hours to play.

Carissa was showing Liu Xiang some of her scrolls.

"Here. Have this one. It is a Greek, Latin, Chinese basic lexicon. I've been working on it for some time."

"No. You have put a lot of work into it. You must keep it."

"It's ok. I make a copy of all my work. Here, let me help you with your Greek."

Carissa went over the Greek sounds with Liu Xiang. She taught him some of the Greek aphorisms and sayings that children learnt in their lessons all across the spreading Roman Empire. Liu Xiang's favorite was from a man called Pericles. "What you leave behind is not what is carved in stone, but what is woven into the lives of others."

In return, Liu Xiang taught Carissa some Chinese Idioms that she didn't know. Her favorite was "Four things come not back: the spoken word, the spent arrow, the past life, and the neglected opportunity." She could not help laughing at the last one she was told as Liu Xiang ran his fingers through his thinning hair. "Experience is a comb that we are given only after we have lost most of our hair."

The travelers made shelters amongst the trees and slept. Bing kept watch. After some time Liu Xiang came out to him.

"I will take over."

"No. You should sleep."

"We must all play our part."

"But you're ..."

"Old?"

"Well. Yeah."

"So respect your elders and do what I say."

Liu Xiang sat next to Bing around the fire. They stared into the dance of reds and oranges and blues. The smoke comforted them as it swirled around them.

"I know who killed your family Bing."

Bing had almost fallen asleep but he sat up hearing those words.

Liu Xiang said, "I know. But I'm not going to tell you."

"Why?"

"I'll tell you when you are ready."

"I want to know."

"No. You must focus on your family. You still need to think about them. To feel the joy of them as well as the pain."

"I want to know."

"You want to know so you can be angry. That won't help you right now."

"Why did you tell me you knew?"

"To prepare you for when I do tell you. So that you know I'm not keeping a secret from you, but will one day tell you."

"I ... I ... want to know."

Liu Xiang looked at Bing.

"No, you're right. I don't. I don't want to think about it at all."

"Lie down now Bing. Think about your family, the good and the bad. Remember them, mourn them. Rest."

Bing wanted to argue but he was tired. He thanked Liu Xiang and curled up in the tent. He missed his family but he was remembering happy times as he fell asleep.

The next day they descended the mountain and came to a plain. Many of the travelers thought they were over the Pamir ranges.

"No," said Liu Xiang. "This is just one of the valleys. It is good because it is flat, but there are more mountains and glaciers to come. You can just make them out through the mist."

The flat plain was easier going and there were small rock and plaster buildings spaced across the landscape that provided shelter. Most of them were shrines of various sorts. Liu Xiang said that Buddhism was becoming popular and that more and more travelers were praying to Buddha for safe travel. Liu Xiang mused on how a prophet had taken on the attributes of a god. There were other shrines and statues of other gods which Bing did not recognize.

After a night on the plain, the travelers made their way up the next mountain. They went as far as they could before dusk and then set up camp. All the travelers slept soundly. They were exhausted.

Bing was woken by lightning and the sound of people packing up their tents. It was time to move on.

They walked on through a light rain. The mist had cleared a bit. There was snow gathered in drifts. The strong smell of the Pine trees comforted the travelers. When the lightning flashed it lit up the trees and the snow.

As they neared the higher part of the mountains everyone walked closer to each other, huddled together. The cold and the mist were worse now. Lightning flashed and thunder shook the mountain and it felt like the strikes were only a stone's throw in front of them.

The blizzard hit. The storm raged and sleet slashed the group. They could hear howls. There had to be something other than the wind. The travelers were scared.

"How do you kill a dragon? Especially one that you cannot see?"

"You can't fight it."

"Let's huddle together. It can't eat all of us at once."

Arrow yelled, "There are no such things as dragons."

The mists rose. Ice and snow cut down on the travelers. They heard a roar. Everything was white and black at the same time. Something was attacking them. They huddled together but roars surrounded them. They felt something brush by them. Sometimes furry, sometimes cold like iron .

"Ahhh ... it's cut my leg ... my leg ... help!" yelled one of the travelers. There was a scream that ended abruptly.

This is it thought Bing. Killed by an invisible dragon. There were other screams, the sound of biting and growling. But then a light came from the east. It was a bright star on the horizon. The mist started to clear. There in front of them, were three white leopards snarling. A man stood behind them in an iron mask. The mask was covered in long spikes. The man had the leopards on chains and had a large spear which he was using to jab and control the leopards.

The star shone brighter and brighter. Everyone stopped and stared at it. Now they could see the dragon for what it really was. A man and his pets. Arrow shot his arrows into the leopards. It made them thrash and they ran away. The man in the mask could not control them. The man remained silent. He stared at the travelers. No one knew what he would do next. He muttered some gibberish and ran at them, he threw his spear at them, piercing one of the travelers. The masked man drew his sword and screamed at the travelers. Swinging his sword at them, the light from the star reflected in his blade and flashed into his eyes. He had blinded himself and he lost his balance. He tripped and slipped over the edge of the mountain. Sliding down, the leopards gathered around him and started attacking him, eating him.

"We had better be going. He is too far down the mountain to do anything," said Liu Xiang.

The travelers found a rock dwelling ahead. It was a rock structure, like a small castle. Lamps were burning inside and there were carvings of dragons around the walls. Surrounding the castle were tamarisk trees, flowering pink.

"It is a special flower that appears, even in the bitter cold of winter," said Liu Xiang. Butterflies flew around the flowers and their beauty had a calming effect on the travelers.

They dressed the wounds of those who had been cut by the leopards. They buried one slave that had been killed. They decided to spend the night inside until the blizzard passed completely.

Liu Xiang was excited. "The star has appeared. As I expected, it is a broom star. This star symbolizes God sweeping away evil. We will follow it on our quest for peace." Everyone cheered.

Despite all this talk of peace, Jacob and Bing talked about fighting. They discussed technique and their theories on training. Arrow kept trying to interrupt but Carissa kept telling him to be quiet.

"Right now we are learning about real fighting. If we want to learn about archery we will ask you."

Arrow poked his tongue out at her. He turned to the Xiongnu and talked with them. It was strange. He spent so much of his time learning to hate the Xiongnu but they really had a lot in common.

When the blizzard had subsided, the travelers made their way down the Western side of the mountains. It was arduous. But the star woke them every morning and it encouraged them to keep trudging along.

CHAPTER EIGHT

They came to the base of the mountains and were exhausted but they couldn't rest for long. The land stretched out Westward in front of them and they had to keep going to keep up with the star. It appeared in the early morning and even when they couldn't see it during the day they walked in the direction that it had been pointing.

It was good to be walking on flat ground. The downward slopes of the mountain had been even worse than the ascent.

The environment was changing. It began to look like farming land again. Although the land was flat the weather did not help their progress. In the mornings it was cold, and then in the afternoon it would warm up but then it would rain.

There were not many traveler stops but the people who lived in the area were hospitable. They smiled and gave the travelers food and advice. They warned them of the weather and that there may soon be floods. The people spoke a kind of Greek that was sometimes difficult to understand. Carissa spoke to them in one of the Persian dialects.

The flood hit when the travelers were not expecting it. At that time it was not raining where they were walking but they could see the grey clouds over the mountains behind them and they saw the grey expanse of rain that connected the ground to the clouds. Liu Xiang sent Arrow up a tall tree to report on the situation.

"Quick," yelled Arrow, from up the tree. "We must keep walking. The waters are rising and heading in our direction."

Up ahead of them was a tall hill and beyond them another hill. On the top of the second hill were trees, their roots winding down, intertwined in rocks.

Liu Xiang looked back at the waters running towards them. He observed the two hills.

"Everyone. Listen. We must get to the further hill. It is sturdier, safer." Liu Xiang tried to warn everyone and Carissa helped him spread the message.

Some of the travelers didn't heed the warnings, they ran up the closer, sandy hill. Liu Xiang beckoned them to keep going but they didn't listen. The others followed Liu Xiang and pushed on to the hill further away even though they were tired.

They walked to the top, climbing over the rocks and trees. The waters arrived and were swirling around both hills. The first hill started to dissolve. It had just been a mound of sand and dirt, blown together over the years, but this flood was testing it.

"What can we do?" asked Bing.

"Nothing," said Liu Xiang. "Unless they can swim, those who didn't listen will drown."

A few of the travelers who had climbed the first hill were able to swim across to the rocky hill and climb up. The others were sucked away into the swirling, raging waters.

Everyone lay on top of the hill, under the trees. They had time to catch their breath as the waters went down. Arrow looked around the edges. He pulled out his crossbow. "There are some good fish in there."

Everyone looked at Arrow. He looked like he knew what he was doing. Arrow smiled at the attention.

"I used to be a fisherman before the King called me. This little instrument has always been useful," he said, holding up the crossbow. He had a tool that could attach a sturdy string to the crossbow bolt. He pierced fish after fish and reeled them in. Everyone sat and ate the fish that Arrow caught.

Liu Xiang and Bing sat, ate and talked. "How is your heart?" asked Liu Xiang.

"It desires revenge," said Bing.

"You know that he who desires revenge should first prepare two graves," said Liu Xiang.

"Isn't there justice in revenge?"

"Let me see your son's stick."

Bing handed Bao's small, twisted walking stick to Liu Xiang.

"It's twisted but it still helped Bao walk."

"Yes," said Bing. "All the wood was twisted. We couldn't find any stick that was completely straight."

"Why didn't you cut this one? Shave it, so that it was straight?"

"We wanted Bao to know that being twisted was normal."

"It is normal. If you look around. Everyone is twisted in some way. It is normal, but is it good?" Liu Xiang handed the stick back to Bing.

"Are you twisted in any way Bing?" asked Liu Xiang.

"Well, Confucius said that all are born good. That people are essentially good. That may be the case for everyone else, but if I'm honest, I'm the exception to that rule."

"Why do you say that?"

"I've never been able to have completely righteous thoughts, since as long as I can remember. I know what's in my heart and it scares me."

"Your desire for revenge scares you?"

"Yes."

"Good. Remember. If you are patient in your day of anger, you will save a hundred days of regret." Liu Xiang stood up and threw his fishbone back into the water. Then he lay down for a rest. Bing sat against one of the trees and looked back at the mountains they had travelled over.

After a few days the group was able to walk again once the ground had dried out. They had more energy after their enforced rest. They plodded West and the land became desert again, they kept going and there were patches of green watered by irrigation trenches from the North.

They passed traveler rest stops and traded their mules in for camels. The people were not as hospitable as before and were more interested in the wares or gold that the travelers possessed.

Liu Xiang sent many of the servants away. They needed to move swiftly to keep up with the star. Also, too large a group would attract unwanted attention. Some of the travelers put on servants clothes so they did not look rich and conspicuous. They didn't want to look like royalty. They made sure they only looked like servants, merchants or priests.

"These prices are crazy," Carissa would complain at the food stalls but then she would turn back to the group and wink. She was only saying that so that the food sellers would give her a better deal. Her beauty mixed with her mock anger got them a lot of cheap food.

At one of the traveler stops, riders came to the group. The riders looked confused. They were Parthian but did not look menacing like the Parthian guards that kept checking them at each rest stop.

"Are you merchants or spies?" asked one of the riders in Greek.

"We are envoys from various countries. We seek safe

passage through your land," said Liu Xiang in Greek. Carissa winked at him.

"Where are you going?"

"We don't know. We have a map that we are following."

"Show us the map."

Liu Xiang pointed up at the sky. "We will wait till night."

One of the riders whispered something to the leader.

"Don't worry, we are not a threat," said Liu Xiang in Parthian. The riders tilted their head at him. Carissa smirked. "I didn't know you knew Parthian," she said.

"Just that one line," whispered Liu Xiang.

"We will take you to Hecatompylos. There is someone there who we think will want to meet you."

Carissa turned to Arrow. "Do you think there is any danger going with them?"

"No. And I'm here to protect you if you need me," said Arrow.

Carissa ignored him.

"You have been thinking about something recently," said Carissa.

"Just you," said Arrow.

"No. That's not true," said Carissa. "It is about Bing. You are worried about him."

Arrow said nothing. He looked back at Bing. He was at the back of the group talking with Jacob.

"I have a nickname. Actually, people use it as an insult but I'm not insulted," said Jacob.

"What is it?" asked Bing.

"My Jewish friends and family call me Porky. You know, like Pig?"

"That's a good thing in China."

"Yeah. Well not in Judaism. Pigs are unclean you know."

"Unclean? What do you mean? They're cute ... and delicious."

"Yeah, I know. I love eating pig. That's why my people don't like me. But you know what? We think you Chinese eat disgusting things. Pigs I like, but some of that other stuff. I'm not a fan. Eating Pig's blood. Errgh!"

" Do you want to know my nickname?"

"Let me guess. Super warrior?"

"No. They call me Halfie. Because I'm half Han Chinese and half Korean. I like it, but it too is used as an insult."

"Why?"

"Because people think that one's blood should be pure."

"Chinese and Korean are the same aren't they? You all look the same."

Some of the travelers turned and glared at Jacob.

"I'm just joking," said Jacob

Everyone looked away.

"My people are paranoid about our pure blood too," said Jacob to Bing. "No one is pure though. Don't you think?"

"Yeah. What color is your blood?" asked Bing.

"What?"

"What color is your blood. I heard that non-Chinese people have different colored blood."

"Are you crazy? Everyone's blood is the same."

"Prove it."

Jacob looked at Bing then Bing laughed.

"I'm just joking."

"Ha! Blood might be the same, but our sense of humor is different."

CHAPTER NINE

The travelers were blown towards Hecatompylos by the wind and sand. They approached a big gate in the wall made out of dirt. The dirt had been molded and leveled so it looked like brick. There were palm trees around the large walls and torches burning along the top of the walls even in daylight.

"Where are the other gates?" asked Arrow. Liu Xiang smiled at him. Carissa put her hand on Arrow's shoulder.

"City of a hundred gates. The gates aren't literal, just symbolic. This is where people meet and interact from the ends of the earth, a lot like Kashi."

"Just more civilized," said the Parthian rider.

"Civilized means different things to different people," said Liu Xiang in Chinese.

"What did he say?" asked the Parthian rider.

"That the city is beautiful," said Carissa.

They entered the city gates and indeed it reminded Bing of Kashi. There was an even greater mix of people and the smells and colors in the marketplace were even more diverse. Bing closed his eyes and let the smells work on his imagination: cumin mixed with chili mixed with dill mixed with rosewater mixed with barbecue smoke mixed with incense mixed with the aroma of baked bread. They headed North towards the palace, and before they got there a man in flowing silk robes ran towards them.

"Exotic travelers. You have arrived just in time. I almost left yesterday but had to advise some of the plumbers on fixing the palace pipes. There was the smell of excrement all through the palace till only this morning."

The man ran and welcomed everyone. It was an absurd sight, this man looked too dignified to run, too dignified to bow to them, but he was clearly excited. The big ball of a hat on his head made him look like a clown, thought Bing. Liu Xiang was amazed at the man's Chinese.

"Some of my contacts told me about you when they saw you on the road. You are all so brave. Travelling is so dangerous these days. Come. I will show you my charts," said the man.

Liu Xiang smiled. He knew what the man was going to tell him.

"Oh by the way, my name is Pej. I'm the King's city planner and map maker. I love cities, I love maps. All kinds of maps, especially maps of the heavens. So come this way. I love this place in Winter."

"You have it to yourself?"

"Yes. Apart from the guards and servants, and commoners, and merchants and the other priests and scholars who are stationed here. The royal family are in Ctesiphon right now. It is a good thing too as they probably wouldn't have given you a great welcome."

"They want to protect their trade route and think we would be a threat?"

"Exactly."

"You are so wise and kind."

"Thanks."

"Here, come and check this out."

On a large table Pej had maps and charts laid out.

"Here come see!"

"Let me guess ... the star in the East that appeared over

a week ago is going to lead you to a King."

"How did you know I was going to say that?"

"Lucky guess."

"I was going to go on behalf of the King and present a gift. I haven't told any of the other Priests or Scholars. Even Phraates doesn't know anything about it. I was going to do it without him knowing."

"Why's that?"

"Most Kings don't like other Kings. But if we don't respect this new King I fear that we will be destroyed."

"Tell me more," said the astronomer of Wa.

Pej told Liu Xiang and Wa all that he knew about the new King, bringing in sources from local historical, scientific and religious writings.

"He's going to be a Jewish King. From Jerusalem," said Pej looking around cautiously. Then he said, "Oh I need a rest." He lent backwards with his hands on his hips to stretch his back and neck. "Hey, you're from China aren't you? Have you got one of those new gong thingamajigs?" asked Pej.

Liu Xiang smiled. "I do. Just a small one." Liu Xiang took out a small metal gong from one of his packs and a wooden mallet. He set it up for Pej, hanging it on a small wooden stand.

"Great," said Pej. These are becoming very popular on the trade routes. He struck the gong. Everyone covered their ears because it was so loud. "Oh, this is fun. This size would make a handy throwing weapon too wouldn't it?"

Liu Xiang nodded.

Arrow, Bing, Jacob and Carissa sat at the doorway.

"I still don't understand," said Bing. "If the King is only just going to be born, how much good will he be as a child. Shouldn't we wait until he's twelve or so? Isn't that the time for visiting?"

"It's always good to act quickly," said Carissa looking at Arrow.

Pej looked towards the group at the door.

"This is a powerful supernatural King. When he comes he will conquer all in his way ... and I mean all. We must make sure we are on his good side. I'm sure his father is already very influential," said Pej.

"Fair enough," said Arrow.

Jacob stood up. "Do you really want to know what this is all about ... apparently? I don't believe in any of it but I have an idea about what you are looking for and I think you will be interested. Pej is wrong when he said the King will be born in Jerusalem, no offence."

Pej made a mock offended face.

"How do you know so much?" asked Pej.

"My father was a Rabbi," said Jacob.

"I see. Jerusalem is where the King of the Jews lives and governs. That's where the temple is. But you say this new King will be born somewhere else? Prove it," said Pej and he hit the gong for dramatic effect. Everyone covered their ears again.

"Does someone have a copy of Micah's scroll?" asked Jacob.

Pej jumped up and down with his hands in the air. "Oh yes! I do. Wait here. I have the whole collection. Come and help me Carissa."

They ran off together and came back, each with an armful of scrolls.

"Just asked for the one," said Jacob. And he opened up the scrolls and he taught them about what it said about the Jewish King or Messiah, although he himself believed none of that nonsense.

CHAPTER TEN

With high spirits, the travelers headed South Westward for Ctesiphon near Babylon. Travelling with Pej brought a lot of energy and opportunity to the group. The roads were getting busier. The Parthians liked getting their cut from the trade routes and certain traders weren't allowed in certain areas. Pej was always able to sweet talk or bribe the guards that tried to stop them. He didn't want to use his royal seal too much because he wasn't officially on royal business.

"The King will be heading to Rhagae for the Spring. We may pass him on the way. We will have to be careful if we do, he may feel threatened by all of you and feed you to his lions. We will regroup at Ctesiphon, make our calculations and go from there," said Pej.

The journey west of Hecatompylos was uneventful at first. There were many merchants joining them or passing them on the road. There was always interesting food to buy and clothes and animals and weapons that Bing had never seen before in his life. Jacob wanted everyone to buy and wear the big funny puffy hats like Pej wore but no one would go along with him.

They sent a scout towards Rhagae who reported that

the Royal banners were up in the city and that the royal family had arrived. They camped at a distance and then waited to pass the city just before dawn when the guard would have been at its most lax. They passed and it didn't look like anyone at the city noticed. They continued on their journey until Pej noticed that one of his servants had left them and headed back towards the city.

"Probably one of Musa's slippery spies. She is a true Medusa, eyes everywhere. I think she is dangerous too. Even Phraates should be careful around her."

A group of horsemen were riding towards them from the city. They did not look friendly. The travelers picked up their pace but the riders were gaining quickly.

"Quick," Arrow said to Bing. "Get Jacob and we will block the archers." The Wa warriors and the Xiongnu looked ready to help.

They heard a terrifying sound. A sand twister had risen up in front of their party and it was bearing towards them. It was not huge but it scared the travelers. They fell to the ground in fear. Should they run to the North or to the South. The twister was weaving its way towards them ... they couldn't tell which way it was going.

"It's no use, we'll be trapped either way," said Bing as he looked at the approaching pillar of sand and back towards the archers on horseback.

The twister bore down on them but as if intentionally it veered from its course and headed towards the Parthian Royal guard, it slammed into them, picking them off their horses and sent them flying.

"Let's keep moving," said Liu Xiang.

"Forward!" said Pej.

They pushed on through the dust and sand. Giant dunes slouched around them like sleeping animals. No one else from the Royal party came back to bother them. They continued travelling from town to town as fast as they could.

When they rested, everyone would stare up at the sky.

The scholars would discuss the movements of the stars and their meanings, some of them would wonder at how big the cosmos was and others would talk about home.

There were always arguments when they started talking about religion and philosophy, Buddhism, Hinduism, Shamanism, Taoism, Zoroastrianism, Judaism, the mandate of heaven. They discussed whether there were many gods or just one God. If there was, was it the same God viewed from different perspectives? Jacob even said he didn't think there was such a thing as God and that human reason was the most important thing. Everyone gasped at his belief. Liu Xiang had to calm things down when the discussion got too heated.

They swapped stories of ancient heroes around the fire. Hercules, Nimrod, Rostam, Gilgamesh, David. Jacob gave a moving rendition of Abraham the warrior Prince leading his Army against the enemy Kings and rescuing his whining nephew Lot. He screamed and wailed and whined and had the entire party laughing. Bing laughed with everyone, but inside he was thinking about his family.

The travelers stayed just a short time in Ecbatana to rest and replenish supplies. They were looking forward to resting at the caravan stop near the great rock of Behistun where Darius and others had carved impressive monuments to celebrate their conquests. Instead of the barbecue and foot massages that they craved, there were two small groups of soldiers waiting for them. Roman soldiers blocked the road to their West and some Parthian archers to the East.

The Parthian chief called to Pej.

"Phraates IV demands to know what you are doing. We have orders to bring you home and to give anyone who is not a Parthian to the Roman Soldiers to take as prisoners. We have an agreement with Rome."

Pej looked in fear. Obviously they didn't take the travelers too seriously because there weren't many men, but the soldiers and riders surrounding them were still intimidating.

Pej whispered, trying not to move his mouth too much and said, "The one thing we have in our favor is that they have underestimated us. Firstly, the Romans are only rogue soldiers, using the name of Rome to their advantage. They are nothing more than slave traders. Secondly, there are only twelve archers. If we can stop them, then we already have the upper hand."

"But how will we stop them?" asked Bing.

"Don't look too quickly but when you can, look towards the Eastern hill," said the envoy from Wa.

Bing looked out of the corner of his eye and saw the two female warriors from Wa making their way towards the horseback archers.

"How did they know?" asked Bing.

The envoy of Wa said, "They are trained to go straight to danger. I would suggest that we get ready to fight. They won't wait till we are ready."

And sure enough, Bing saw the women draw their long slender swords and merge into the shadows as they walked towards the archers.

Pej stood up and yelled back at the Parthian chief, "We accept."

The Parthian chief smiled. "You accept our offer? Great. Send the prisoners to the Romans and you come to us."

The travelers walked towards the Romans and Pej walked towards the Parthians with his servants.

"I don't think you understand," said Pej. "We accept your surrender, and we will grant you your lives if you leave now."

The Parthian chief shook his head and nodded to his archers.

"Ok. Shoot when ready."

The Archers drew their bows and aimed at Pej and the other travelers around him. In a blur, closest to the

Western hill, an Archer's head landed on the ground, his body was still sitting up on the horse grasping the bow, and then another head fell to the ground. The other archers sensing what was happening looked towards their comrades.

The Wa warriors quickly and silently detached two more heads with their swords and the archers forgot about their orders. They turned their horses and rode away.

One of the Wa warriors threw three small metal throwing knives at the archers and each one hit a different rider. The three riders slumped and fell.

The other archers, as they rode, turned in their saddles and took up their bows again.

They fired on the two women. One of the women had an arrow pierce her left arm, through the elbow, although she avoided the other two arrows aimed at her. The other woman rolled on the ground, evading four arrows, and then got to her feet and threw two small throwing knives shaped like stars. They landed in the head of one of the riders.

The women chased the archers down and were stuck with arrows while they did. The taller of the Wa warriors pulled an arrow out of her stomach. She ran towards the closest rider and used the arrow to stab him. That was her last act before she fell, dead from her wounds. The other warrior too, was not going to survive the wounds that she had received but in one last swing took off the head of one of the last two archers. The last rider, the one who had given the orders was riding away. The three Xiongnu ran, jumped on the Parthian horses that were now riderless and pursued.

Meanwhile, everyone else turned to the Romans. Bing was up for some action. He viewed it as a light workout. Weeks on a camel could really give you sore buttocks.

The Romans were well trained, but there was fear in their ranks when they saw what the two women had done to the Parthian archers. They weren't expecting to fight so soon. They clustered together, putting their shields up.

"Looks like the time to use this. Picked it up from the markets," said Liu Xiang and he took out a ball wrapped in cloth from his pack. He unwrapped the ball and scratched a stick on the rock next to him, creating a flame. Liu Xiang lit the string attached to the ball and it started sparking. Liu Xiang with all his might threw the ball into the middle of the Roman soldiers. The ball exploded. The Soldiers on the inside were on fire. The ones around the rim were not waiting to see if they too were flammable. They ran for the travelers with their shields and swords in front of them.

Bing hadn't seen Jacob fight in a real battle before and he was impressed. Jacob twirled and jabbed, methodically moving through the Roman soldiers and making calculated and deadly hits. He grabbed shields and used them against the Roman soldiers who had been holding them.

Arrow was firing his crossbow bolts between the gaps in the shields. Others of the group were also using whatever weapons they had.

Bing ran and helped Jacob. The Roman soldiers were fighting well together but they were unsure how to defend themselves against such determined opponents. Also, they struggled with the different styles of fighting.

Carissa swung her sword. She was fast. The Roman soldiers were no match for her speed. She moved forward and attacked and then sprang back and rested. Then once more attacked and then sprang back.

Bing looked across at Liu Xiang. He too was fighting. He looked like he was seventeen. He swayed from side to side with grace and poise, swinging his blade like he was dancing.

Bing didn't need to unsheathe his own sword. He punched a Roman soldier in the ribs and before he needed to do anything else Carissa had put her sword through the soldier's stomach. Bing kicked a Roman soldier in the kneecap and before he could do anything else Liu Xiang had pierced the Roman soldier's heart through a gap in his breastplate.

The Roman soldiers lay lifeless on the ground after a short time. There were no more casualties amongst the travelers. Liu Xiang looked old again.

Carissa looked to the Astronomer and envoy of Wa.

"Your two women gave their life for us. They knew they weren't going to survive but they didn't even hesitate."

"If determined, a warrior can live beyond their death, performing one more glorious action, even if their head be removed from their body," said the envoy of Wa.

Bing looked at the dead Roman soldiers. He felt no remorse for them. He looked over at the two women who had sacrificed themselves. He and Arrow went, picked up their bodies and brought them back to the group.

The astronomer and envoy of Wa were silent as they buried their two bodyguards.

"It was like they acted without thinking, without fear," said Carissa.

"No," said the envoy of Wa. "In their training they learn to endure both physical and emotional pain. They were fully aware that they were going to die. That is what makes their actions courageous." The group was silent.

After a while Pej broke the silence.

"Just as I mentioned," Pej said. "You are all very brave to make this journey with me. Thank you."

The Xiongnu arrived back. They had taken care of the rider. There would be no one to report to the Parthian King.

The travelers walked up to where the Roman prisoners were. Most of the prisoners ran away when released but one of the prisoners, Philo, stayed. Liu Xiang started a conversation with him.

Philo called himself a Jewish Roman. He had been captured for apparently being a threat to Herod. He said he had killed a lot of Romans. He was a freedom fighter or more to the point, he was fighting for the Kingdom of

God.

Jacob said he was a crazy zealot. Philo and Jacob hated each other the second they saw each other.

"You look like someone who doesn't take the Law of God seriously," said Philo.

"You look like someone who doesn't take life seriously," Jacob spat back.

But Philo was impressed with Liu Xiang's Greek skills. Liu Xiang asked him to join the group. He may even have Philo teach him Aramaic or Hebrew if there was time. Jacob went away from the group to sulk.

"I will help you. Where are you going?" asked Philo.

"We are looking for a new King. Apparently the one who will be born King of the Jews," said Liu Xiang looking at Pej and then Jacob.

"The Messiah. The last Messiah I followed, now he was crazy. When I followed him I fought and killed so many Romans. I think I killed 200 of them myself," said Philo.

"You're joking?" said Carissa

"I swear on Moses' big toe, that I am not," said Philo.

"What happened to this Messiah?" asked Liu Xiang.

"The Romans cut his tongue out and crucified him. Wasn't pretty," said Philo.

"But you escaped?" asked Carissa.

"Yeah. I'm invincible," said Philo.

Everyone laughed including Philo. He joined the travelers and together they marched towards Ctesiphon. They travelled via a shortcut that Philo was familiar with. They passed through rocky passages and there were many who looked like bandits, hiding in the mountains, but Philo went before them and no one bothered the travelers.

CHAPTER ELEVEN

They arrived at Ctesiphon. The star had already passed over them in the night sky. It was before them, in the direction of Jerusalem, just as Pej had said it would be. Pej gave Jacob a smug smile.

Ctesiphon felt like a royal city, less of a merchant city compared with Hecatompylos or Kashi. It was a less practical city, built to impress. It was constructed over at least three rivers from what Bing could tell. The roads and bridges were sturdy. There was plenty of shopping happening but many of the people walked around the streets in gaudy clothes, not actually doing anything but looking and wanting people to look at them.

The spring air filled Bing with memories of preparing to plant the crops with his family. The pain of loss didn't constantly cut into his heart like a knife, but there was an ache that he tried to push away by pressing his arms to his chest.

"Pej, is that you? I have some things you may like." A boisterous woman rushed up to Pej and gave him a hug.

"Savitri. Good to see you. I thought you would have left by now. Back through Bactria and home. Before things got too hot."

"No, I had a feeling you would be coming this way. I hadn't sold all my goods, so I thought you may be interested. And Pej, I like the heat."

"Everybody, this is Savitri, Queen of the traders. She is one of the richest merchants in the known world," said Pej, changing from Greek to Chinese.

"As well as the wisest and most generous," said Savitri also in Chinese.

Pej laughed. "You are so modest. Now show me what you have."

Pej let them into the palace after making sure that it was safe. The guards weren't too sure what to think but Pej made Savitri give them some of her goods and the guards didn't complain any more.

The travelers felt excited that they had come so far. And this taste of comfort made them think about the new Royal family they would meet in Judea. Maybe there they would be treated to even more luxury.

Savitri had a friend with her. "Meet my bodyguard, Zayin." A large man bowed. He only wore trousers and sandals and nothing else on his chest except for the leather strap that ran from one shoulder to his waist, and held the large sword on his back. He also had throwing knives attached to his belt. Bing counted at least seven.

Everyone sat down and ate and drank. Liu Xiang who always drank copious amounts of tea tried to pour some for everyone. Jacob let everyone try some of his wine. Savitri laid out some cakes and yoghurt and sugar candies.

"I'm not used to drinking tea for pleasure," said Savitri. "It is only used for medicinal purposes back home."

"Oh, you must drink more of it," said Liu Xiang. "It is so good for your whole being. Body and soul."

Pej diluted the tea with some goats milk. "What are you doing?" said Liu Xiang in exasperation.

Savitri smiled at Liu Xiang and said, "I don't think tea will ever be popular where I'm from. Sorry to offend you."

Liu Xiang wasn't offended. He tried to think of something to say. He sipped his tea and said, "I like your bodyguard. I wouldn't wear a shirt either if I had muscles like that ... we have bodyguards too."

"I know. Bodyguards are essential. There are so many bandits and swindlers along the road. It pays to have good people looking after you. Some of these merchants don't listen. They travel in groups of two or three, on the back of camels. And like that ... they get attacked by bandits. No one ever hears of them again," said Savitri.

Liu Xiang was taken by Savitri. He tried out his language skills on her. He had had many interactions with the Bactrian and Hindu traders who visited China.

"Wow, old man. You speak my language so well." She switched to Aramaic. "You really think that this new King is genuine?"

Liu Xiang apologized that he did not know any Aramaic. Savitri was impressed that at least he knew what language she had spoken and then switched to Greek and Liu Xiang nodded and explained about what the sky had told him, the stories that Pej and Jacob had shared and everyone's desire for peace.

"Well, I'm planning on coming with you too. Right this instant, I've made up my mind. Visiting this new King will be good for business. Give him some samples of our stuff. Zayin has introduced me to the wonders of Arabia. Here smell this," said Savitri and offered around some incense and spices for everyone to smell.

"Will you give the child a birthing ceremony?" asked Bing.

Everyone looked at him. Carissa translated and then continued to translate as Bing spoke.

"When our children were born ..." Bing paused and swallowed. "Where we are from, after the child's first year, after the women pray to the gods, asking for blessing. Then you put gifts in front of them ... and the child chooses one of the gifts. That will tell you about their future. What their character will be like."

"Yes. We could see what type of King the boy would be. With Gold, a scroll and some Tea," Liu Xiang said.

"Tea?" What would that tell us?" Asked Philo.

"Ah ... a healing King, perhaps. Gold for a rich King," said Liu Xiang. "A scroll for a wise King."

"How about a sword to see if he will be a mighty warrior," said Carissa.

"Hmmm. Really?" said Arrow.

Everyone talked more. They were happy. The journey and its difficulties seemed faraway in the past. The people that had tried to stop them and the events that had conspired against them did not seem to matter now. On top of that, the servants were pampering them.

One of them was a smiling tall skinny man with so much curly hair that it looked like he was wearing a hat. His name was Adam. He helped the travelers with all their needs and made them feel comfortable. He was pleased that he could accompany them to Jerusalem. He was excited that he could show them his hometown of Damascus, which they would pass through on the way.

Liu Xiang stood up to make an announcement. "Tell everyone to get ready. We leave in a day's time. We need to head North before we can head West into Judea. We need to hurry. We may not be safe here and the star is getting lower every night."

CHAPTER TWELVE

The travelers made their way North. The roads were busy at this time of year and no one wanted trouble. They were leaving Parthian territory now and out of Phraates jurisdiction and obviously no one missed the Roman soldiers that had attacked them. As long as the travelers did not draw attention to themselves they could blend in with the merchants and pilgrims that were everywhere on the road.

At Damascus, Adam took them into the city and first showed them Chinatown. Wow, thought Liu Xiang. He hadn't even heard of it. But it was such a good idea. A tiny part of the city amongst the silk stalls where they made everything look like Chang'an. It had been set up by the small number of Chinese that had made it this far West. The food was terrible. It had been modified for the local taste, but Bing closed his eyes and the smells took him back to China.

"Now, Men, come and enjoy the springs at the bathhouse," said Adam. He took them to his house where they left their goods and weapons. The women stayed behind to rest. The ladies' baths were closed for renovation.

The men followed Adam. As they walked further into the middle of the city, the streets becoming narrower. They were away from the crowded streets full of people and noise. Adam took them through a door into a large enclosed courtyard and they could see that there was a well in the middle. They heard groans and what sounded like screams, but they couldn't tell where it was from.

"What are those noises?" asked Arrow.

"We are very close to the hospital," said the smiling man. "Please, have a drink from the sacred well before we continue on."

Everyone huddled around the well.

"Does anyone have some rope on hand?" asked Adam. "I need it for the bucket. So silly of me to forget."

"I have some, somewhere," said one of the other travelers.

"Never mind. I have some over here." Adam went back, walked through the door and closed it.

Men started climbing out of the well, or people who had once been men. Now, their skin was peeling and they had a crazed look in their eyes. They drooled and screamed. And they walked intently towards the travelers.

"Demoniacs!" yelled Jacob, "Watch out everyone!"

Bing tried to open the door that Adam had slammed. It was no use.

Bing, Arrow, Jacob, Philo, Zayin, Pej and the other men looked at each other. They had to fight these creatures. Some of the drooling, vacant eyed men had chains wrapped around them which they spun and hurled towards the travelers.

There were twelve of these demoniacs. They were hooting and yelling. It made Bing shiver. What had happened? Why were they being attacked by these ... men.

"I know it looks easier to kill them than to capture them. But somewhere in there they are still themselves. We have to knock them out. We have to bind them somehow," said Jacob.

"We don't have our weapons, anyway," said Bing.

"But we can break their necks," said Arrow.

"No. We can bind them," said Jacob.

Philo nodded.

"As much as anyone I want to rip these monsters apart." Philo said. "But Porky is right. Part of them is still them."

"Ah. It would be so much easier just to kill them," said Arrow under his breath.

The monstrous men ripped and grabbed at Liu Xiang and the others. Bing managed to wrestle the chain away from one man and tie it around him. But the man flexed and the chain disintegrated.

One of the men bit into Arrow's arm. Arrow shouted in pain as he pulled free.

Liu Xiang moved slowly. He used the frantic movements of the demoniacs to his advantage. He would walk near a wall and then move out of the way just as one of the demoniacs would lunge at him. The demoniac would slam into the wall and be stunned for a moment.

Bing was fighting back to back with Arrow who was trying to tie up his arm to stop the bleeding.

Bing was doing flying kicks, trying to knock out the attackers but nothing was working. The deranged men would just get back up again.

The travelers were weary, they felt like these screaming, yelling, jerking men would tear them to pieces. Their strength and relentlessness were not natural.

"Stop!" A barely discernible voice echoed around the walls in Aramaic. There was music from lightly strummed strings.

An old lady climbed out of the well, holding a small harp. Carissa and Savitri were with her, supporting her.

"In the name of the Lord on high, be calm." The lady was small and frail, but her voice soothed the deranged men. One of them spoke.

"Old lady, you are not strong. You cannot control us."

"Of course I cannot control you. It is not in my strength, or by my authority that I command you to be still."

"You don't know what you are doing," growled another. "We have been commanded to ..."

"I don't want to know what you think you are doing," said the old lady. "Go now!"

"But we must stop these men, we must devour the child ..."

"Enough!" said the lady. "Lord most high, tell these spirits to depart and never return ..."

"We're no listening to you."

"I'm not talking to you," said the old lady. "Please Lord. We are your humble servants. We need your grace and power and courage."

The men started howling and writhing.

"Noooooohhh!!!" the men yelled, but their yelling quickly ceased and they lay, exhausted on the ground.

The lady went to the door and unlocked it with a key.

"Some of you go. Go and find Adam," said the lady. "The rest of you, follow me to the synagogue."

In the outer court of the synagogue, under the eaves, the men lay as some priests and doctors cared for them. They were given food and drink. Grapes, sweet apples and wine. There were even pieces of cheese with a light drizzle of honey on them. Bing turned up his nose at the sour smell of the cheese, but he didn't want to appear rude.

The old lady, whose name was Agathae, was dressing Arrow's wound.

Arrow looked worried and said, "It bit me. Is it poison?"

Agathae looked straight into Arrow's eyes. "You will become like one of them when the sun goes down. I should kill you now."

Arrow's face drained of color and Agathae started laughing. Arrow realized she was joking.

Liu Xiang asked Agathae what this thing called a synagogue was. Agathae said, "We have many older people who cannot travel the long distance to Jerusalem, so our rabbis have encouraged us to have local places to worship and pray."

"Are these places in every city?" asked Liu Xiang.

"No. Not yet. But they are becoming more popular. When people visit us here in Damascus they seem to like the idea."

Liu Xiang and Agathae looked towards the doorway, they heard a loud shout.

Philo and Jacob had caught Adam and they brought him to the synagogue. He spat in Agathae's face. She didn't flinch.

"Poor Adam. He did what he did, because we said we would not take control of him. But you have forced us to enter him. It is your fault Prophetess!" said someone from inside Adam.

The man flung out his arms, and Philo and Jacob who had been holding on were thrown into the air. They landed with a thud against the walls. They were a little bruised and shocked but fine.

"Go now! Leave this city. You know you are not allowed here anymore." Agathae pointed in the direction of the city gate.

The man who once was Adam looked at everyone and laughed.

"You won't survive your journey. You don't even have any idea why you are here. And as for you!" The man pointed at Arrow. "When are you going to tell your friend that you are responsible for having his family murdered?" There was more laughter and the man ran off, lurching and shaking, scraping his fingernails against the brick walls.

Bing's face drained of color. "That's not true is it?" asked Bing.

Arrow looked down. "It is true," he said. "Orders from the Emperor."

"Why?" Bing stood up. He reached for his sword. He wanted to pull it out of its sheath and stab Arrow through the heart. He gripped the sword handle and pulled it, but it was stuck.

"I polished it only yesterday," Bing shouted. "Why is it stuck?" He gave up trying to pull out the sword and whacked Arrow over the head. Arrow made no attempt to duck but bore the blow. Blood appeared on his temple.

"Forgive me," Arrow said, looking down.

"Impossible. IMPOSSIBLE!" Bing turned and ran.

Liu Xiang held up his arm and everyone stood where they were. Liu Xiang went to find Bing.

CHAPTER THIRTEEN

Bing was lying in a corner on the cushions in the room where they were storing their possessions. Liu Xiang walked near him and squatted.

Bing was crying. He was heaving with grief.

"I want to die," said Bing. "I will kill myself."

"I need you to live Bing," said Liu Xiang.

Bing rocked back and forth. "Why? And all this time ..."

Liu Xiang stared out the window. The sun was starting to disappear behind the mountains.

"You're confused. You have so many questions, none of it makes sense."

"Yes. It is so stupid. So much pain."

"Emperors are silly creatures aren't they? The Emperor is supposed to rule with justice and compassion. Confucius, Mencius ... the other wise men, say the Emperor is supposed to bear the guilt of the people, not pour on more and more guilt."

"How can you work for that ... that ... monster?"

"We all have to work together Bing. I did what I can. I'm doing what I can ... what I think is right, perhaps to be a good influence."

"I just want to kill Arrow."

"I know. You have anger inside you. Forgiveness is difficult."

"Forgiveness is impossible."

"When you choose to forgive ... it is you who bears the pain. That's what forgiveness is."

Bing felt exhausted. "Arrow must die. He must."

Liu Xiang looked at the ground. "Vengeance will not help you."

Bing ached. His teeth were chattering as he cried.

"Arrow will be judged one day," said Liu Xiang.

"Why? How do you know that?"

Liu Xiang didn't say anything.

"After we visit the new King, then I will kill Arrow," said Bing.

Liu Xiang stood up and left the room. Carissa walked in and said, "Arrow is sorry."

"Don't defend him," said Bing.

"I'm not. I don't want to ever see him again. I just know he's sorry for what he did."

"He's just sorry because the Emperor turned on him too. But he hasn't lost what I've lost."

"I know."

There was a shout from outside.

"Come quick. Arrow is on the battlements."

Carissa ran out. Bing didn't want to look, but after a few more sobs he felt numb and he dragged himself outside.

The sky was dark now, no moon, just stars.

Arrow was standing on top of a tall tower.

"I'm sorry Bing. I'm going to kill myself." Arrow had his loaded crossbow pointed at his forehead.

Bing yelled back, "Fine. Do it."

Liu Xiang walked up to Bing and hugged him. Bing cried. Liu Xiang whispered in his ear. "Forgive."

"I can't. I can't."

"See what happens when you do."

Liu Xiang took the small stick that was strapped to Bing's leg and gave it to Bing. Bing held his son's small crutch and cried and cried. Bing stopped crying and stood up straight. He held up his hand to Arrow.

"Wait. Don't!"

"No! I deserve death."

"I know. I forgive you ..." As he said the words, his heart burned. But he didn't waver. "I forgive you."

Arrow yelled a long cry and it echoed off the city walls. Everyone below thought that Arrow was yelling just before he killed himself. But he didn't kill himself. He sat down and wept. He rocked back and forward and wept. Carissa and Jacob went to scale the wall to help Arrow down but Liu Xiang told them to stop and he looked at Bing. "You must get him."

"No," said Bing.

"Trust me," said Liu Xiang.

Bing looked up at Arrow huddled on the ledge. He climbed up the wall slowly. Arrow looked at him and he saw the look of pain in Bing's eyes.

"I was just following orders," said Arrow.

"That's all I'm doing now," said Bing. Bing helped Arrow down the wall but he didn't look at him. When they got to the ground, Bing took off the bracelet that he wore to remind him of his family. He gave it to Arrow. "I don't need this to remember them," said Bing. "I want you to wear it." Bing turned and walked away.

Liu Xiang laid out the Wei Qi table so that he and Bing could play a game. It would take Bing's mind off things for a bit. Bing was scowling at everyone and kicking furniture but he agreed to play. He sat down and Jacob brought him some of his wine.

Bing didn't know if Liu Xiang was going senile, or if he had some secret plan but Bing was easily getting the upper hand in the game.

"You know. When I was young, I learnt about forgiveness the hard way," said Liu Xiang.

"What happened?" asked Bing.

"Someone killed my parents, and in the name of justice I hunted down who did it."

"But justice is good, isn't it?" asked Bing.

"Yes. But it is difficult to administer justice, when you are full of anger. I did more damage than good, hunting down my parents' killer."

"And you forgave them? The killer?"

"No I killed them."

"But I thought you said you learnt to forgive."

"Not exactly. I learnt about forgiveness. The killer's daughter forgave me. I killed her father."

"But he deserved justice. He deserved it."

"It didn't make her forgiveness any less special."

They kept putting their pieces down. Bing was surrounding all of Liu Xiang's black pieces with his white pieces. He was almost ready to remove a whole lot of Liu Xiang's pieces and claim victory.

"I can't picture you as an angry young man. You are so wise," said Bing.

"Many old men were once young and angry."

Liu Xiang put another piece down. Bing placed his next stone. He was a few moves away from victory.

"Yes. I have succeeded," said Liu Xiang and put a piece on the board, away from all the other pieces.

"What?" said Bing. He looked at the board. He was definitely still in control. "But your losing."

"That depends on my purpose for playing. I have succeeded in helping you to calm down."

"Thank you," said Bing.

"Now get some rest. Tomorrow we leave for Jerusalem."

Liu Xiang walked off and Jacob sat with Bing and poured him another drink.

Agathae the Prophetess found Liu Xiang at the top of the tower looking up at the stars.

She asked him about his journey. He told her about all their adventures. Savitri joined them on the roof. Liu Xiang was shaking his head.

"I don't know if the journey has been worth it. I'm questioning why we are even here. People have died. We haven't even achieved anything. And after we meet the King ... if we meet the King ... then what?" said Liu Xiang.

"It sounds like the dragon has tried to stop you on more than one occasion," said Agathae.

"We have not come up against any dragons," said Liu Xiang. "Not real ones anyway."

"No. The dragon is real, although not flesh and blood. His weapons are not sword and arrow. He attacks you with lies. His claws are poisoned lies. He rips at your heart and sows doubt. The doubt grows up as weeds, noxious weeds."

"But how do we know anything, if we do not start with doubt?" asked Liu Xiang.

"I'm not talking about doubts and questions. I'm talking about doubt and lies," said Agathae.

"But how can we fight this dragon?" asked Liu Xiang.

"With truth. You cannot hide the truth," said Savitri. "No matter how hard you try to suppress it. You cannot hide it."

"What is truth?" asked Liu Xiang.

"You will meet him soon enough," said Agathae.

CHAPTER FOURTEEN

The group set out from Damascus. Bing didn't look at anyone. He didn't want to be there. Carissa rode near Bing to comfort him but Bing ignored her. Arrow rode at the back of the group. The travelers had lost some of their zeal. Many of the group had stayed behind in Damascus. The business was good there, there were beautiful women, good food. It was a comfortable and safe place to live.

Leaving Damascus, heading into Judea, the remaining travelers were surprised at the sight of many crosses along the road. They had seen some on their earlier travels, at crossroads with men, even women strung up on planks of wood and on trees. But now the crosses were more common.

Some of the unlucky were groaning, some looked dead and were dead and others looked dead but would now and then heave themselves up to breathe an agonized breath. It made the travelers uneasy.

"Barbarians," said Liu Xiang.

"How do you know they are barbarians?" asked Savitri.

"Not them up there. The people who put them up there," said Liu Xiang.

"Why are some only tied up while some are tied and

have nails through their hands?" asked Bing.

Carissa looked at Bing. "Metal's expensive. They only use nails for people with powerful friends."

The last morning before they headed into Jerusalem everyone gathered around the charts and looked at the dawn sky.

The star couldn't be seen that morning. Liu Xiang said it was probably because of the moon, or sun or something like that. Bing wasn't listening closely.

"Doesn't matter. It has to be Jerusalem," said Pej.

"No, I'm telling you. The prophecies say Bethlehem," said Jacob.

"You don't even believe in it Porky," said Pej. "Anyway, Bethlehem wouldn't make sense. Even if King David was born there it isn't anything now. Just a small village full of sheep. Jerusalem is a grand city. The Temple is something to behold, that and Herod's palace and the mighty arena."

In the dawn light they saw more crosses silhouetted along the road. They found out that Herod was stationed in Jerusalem, although he was planning to leave soon for his mountain fortress.

When they approached Jerusalem and Herod's palace they were impressed.

"This looks civilized," said Liu Xiang. There were grand buildings and bustling streets.

"Woah. That's amazing. Roman and Jewish architecture combined with Greek flourishes. It looks beautiful, doesn't it," said Carissa.

They sent Liu Xiang and Pej to introduce the party to Herod's guards. Herod's chief servant told them to go away and that Herod wouldn't see them.

Liu Xiang said that they had come all the way from the East and wanted to visit the King. He said they had gifts from their homeland. The chief servant disappeared for a long time while the travelers waited outside. When the servant came back he told the group that three of the most important travelers would be admitted. The others would have to organize their own lodging.

Liu Xiang, Pej and Savitri were designated to enter. The envoy from Wa was offended but he didn't let on that he was.

Everyone thought that it was a bit of a letdown to be denied an audience with the King. The surrounding inns were clean and everyone welcomed the rest but they were craving more luxury. Maybe they would be let into the palace later when Herod heard about their mission.

In Herod's palace the servant showed the three guests into a waiting room. The group could hear Herod inside the next room, his personal bathhouse. He spoke in Aramaic, Greek and Latin. He mixed them as he spoke.

"What do they want?" asked Herod. "Are they Kings? What? No? Magicians? No? Scholars?"

"I don't really know," said the servant. "They have come from the East."

"From the East. What else should I put down?" asked the scribe

"You put nothing down. I don't want this recorded until I know what they want?" said Herod.

Herod appeared, He looked older and weaker than they expected after hearing his booming voice. Herod welcomed them and asked the three visitors to follow him to his private theatre. They would talk while they watched some dancing. There were soldiers everywhere. This was one of the most fortified palaces that Pej had ever seen.

Liu Xiang presented the gifts of tea and jade to Herod's servant. He nodded, took the gifts, showed Herod and then took them away.

Liu Xiang, Pej and Savitri talked with Herod during the dancing. The women on the stage were beautiful and they smiled with their lips but not with their eyes. They were wearing silk from China, it's transparency did not leave much to the imagination.

When Pej asked which of Herod's sons would succeed him as King, Herod had his bodyguards grab the three. They were held against the wall.

"Who sent you?" asked Herod. "Which of my sons?"

Liu Xiang spoke. The fact he spoke Greek, perplexed Herod. "We have seen the star in the East. We have come to worship the one who has been born King of the Jews."

"Naturally, we knew the Messiah would be one of your family," said Pej.

Herod had the guards release the three. He summoned his advisors and ordered the three visitors sent out of the palace.

Pej, Savitri and Liu Xiang sat drinking tea. They had found the others at an inn just near the walls of the palace. They heard people in the streets discussing them, the exotic travelers. They heard muffled whispers talking about them, making up rumors from what people had heard, about a new King, a war, a revolution. There was fear and excitement in the marketplace.

"Sorry to interrupt," Carissa said as she came in from outside. "Herod wants to see you again. Actually he's asked for all of us."

Everyone was led to another grand building. This was more like it. It was not part of Herod's palace but it was indeed luxurious. Finally, they were able to relax. They sat and waited for Herod, excited and expectant.

A hooded figure entered. It was Herod. He took off his hood and talked to the travelers. "I need to ask you a question. I don't want my sons to know," said Herod. "They are fighting amongst themselves. And there are others, so many others who want to usurp the Kingdom. Don't tell the Romans about what we have discussed!"

"Yes?" asked Liu Xiang.

"Go to Bethlehem. I want you to go and worship the

new King and then come back and tell me where he is. I want to worship him too."

Liu Xiang studied his face. It made sense that the King was scared to talk about another King when his sons were squabbling. He wasn't sure if Herod was telling the truth.

"We will go and pay tribute then come back and report to you."

"Thank you. I will be at my fortress in Masada. Please go there. And remember, don't tell anyone else about our conversation."

That night, Bing had a dream, a nightmare. He saw the heavens open up and he saw beyond time and space. He saw a mighty dragon chasing a woman holding a baby. The dragon was crazed and angry, destroying all in his path in his desire to devour the child. Bing didn't tell anyone about his dream.

CHAPTER FIFTEEN

The travelers regrouped as they planned to depart. Jacob was smiling at Pej.

Jacob said, "I told you we needed to follow the star. Let's head to Bethlehem."

"No way," one of the other envoys said.

"Bethlehem is not even a royal city."

"I'm going home."

"This was all a joke."

"What did you expect?"

The group was in disarray. Since Herod had not treated them well and then said he didn't know anything about the King, the travelers were worried. Even though Herod had finally shown them some hospitality, more of the travelers said goodbye and left.

Liu Xiang, Pej, Savitri and Zayin, along with Jacob, Carissa and Bing, Philo, a Nepalese nun, the astronomer and the envoy of Wa and one of the Xiongnu were all that remained. They rode towards Bethlehem in silence.

It was still night and the travelers looked down in spirit. Then the star reappeared. They had not seen it for days. The star was hanging over Bethlehem as they approached. The star was pointing straight down at Bethlehem. Bing thought it looked like a glistening sword, hanging in the heavens, more ominous than auspicious. Bing pushed the feeling away, along with the lingering memory of his dream.

There was no gate at the entrance to Bethlehem, just a well. They sat by the well because it was too early to try and find the house. As the sun started to rise they entered the town and saw the star ahead of them.

The star was low in the sky. They felt like they could reach up and grab it. But the sunlight was starting to outshine the star. They walked towards the star and as it disappeared into the morning light they saw that it had been hanging over a dwelling, built into a rocky hill.

They waited outside, shuffling their feet. They could smell animals of all types. They weren't sure about the house. It didn't look very royal. They were tired, they were in a daze. Doubt and expectation were wrestling in their hearts.

When the sun had risen over the mountains, the sounds around the little town become louder. People started their working day.

"Who should go first?" asked Carissa.

"Liu Xiang," said Bing. "He's the oldest."

"No," said Liu Xiang. "I don't think the family living here has seen someone from my country before. Let it be Philo."

"No," said Philo. "Jacob deserves to introduce us. He was the one who knew where to go."

The others nodded.

Jacob looked unsure of himself. He looked around. He breathed deeply and loosened up his neck muscles.

"You're not about to fight anyone, you're just going to introduce us," said Carissa.

"Yeah. OK."

Jacob walked up to the doorway and pulled back the cloth curtain that was hanging down.

"Excuse me?"

"Who are you?" A man appeared from the dark. He spoke in an Aramaic that Jacob could only just understand.

"Um. I am ... we are ..." said Jacob.

"What do you want? Be quiet or you'll wake the baby."

The man took Jacob by the hand and walked him outside. As he did he saw the group of travelers standing there. His eyes widened.

"More unexpected events. Just after everyone else has gone home too."

"We are here to ..." Jacob paused, it felt silly saying it. "We are here to worship the baby ... the King?"

"Of course you are," the man said. "I should have known."

"Is it a problem?" asked Jacob.

"No. Just wait till Maria and the boy wake up. Are you hungry? Wait here."

Everyone looked at each other. They shrugged. The man came out later with a plate of bread and placed it on a small wooden table. The travelers asked the man for his name. It was Joseph. The travelers sat and ate. The bread was fresh and delicious.

Liu Xiang boiled some water and made eggs for everyone. Bing prepared tea. That was the last of it, the rest had been given to Herod.

As they were eating, they heard a baby cry and then whimper, and then the sounds of the baby guzzling milk from his mother's breast. Joseph looked up and grinned.

"He's hungry. They'll be out in a little while."

No one knew what to say. Joseph looked at them all.

"You're probably thinking this is all very strange. Not what you expected. Well I'll tell you what. I've seen many things that were unexpected. Like you lot. You look like you've journeyed from the ends of the earth."

"Some of us are from the Islands where the Sun rises," said the envoy of Wa.

"Great. Sounds like another prophecy being fulfilled.

Got so many questions to ask the teachers ... If only Simeon were still alive." Joseph stared off into space.

"Tell us about your son," said Liu Xiang in Greek.

Joseph looked up. "Sorry, my Greek's not so good," he said in Aramaic.

Carissa translated for them. "Please tell us about your son."

"Oh, my son. Yeah ... my son," said Joseph with a thoughtful expression on his face. "Well. He was definitely unexpected. And ah ... well. Let's just say, there is a lot expected from him. Not just from us, mind you." Joseph looked up at the heavens.

The travelers listened to Joseph describe all that had happened in the last year. The unexpected pregnancy, the unwanted journey to Bethlehem. How they had to stay with the animals under the house and how the baby was born there, with all those who were staying in the house peering down on them. And how shepherds had startled them in the night. They had thought the shepherds were bandits. But they had come in and bowed before the baby and then ran around Bethlehem making so much noise the soldiers in the area came and chased them back to their flocks of sheep which were birthing on the hillside.

"So that's why seeing such an exotic and grand group of travelers does not surprise me in the least," said Joseph. And he lay back as if to indicate he didn't want to speak anymore.

The travelers were impressed with Joseph's humility and his honesty. Joseph looked back at the travelers, amazed by their different faces. He realized that no one was looking at him. They were looking past him towards the entrance to the house.

There was the baby, snuggling into his young mother. She glowed despite looking exhausted.

The travelers felt a surge of emotion. They walked past Joseph and knelt before the baby. Maria started crying.

"Sorry. I'm overwhelmed."

Bing now realized how silly his plan was to see which gift the baby would choose. The travelers presented the gifts to the baby, laying everything at his feet.

Maria was crying and crying. The baby was drunk with milk, looking peaceful and smiling perhaps. It is so difficult to tell with a baby only a few months old what their expression means.

"Please stay with us today and tonight if you need to," said Maria through her tears.

They had a day of playing with the baby and hearing more from Maria about all that had happened.

They said they would stay one more night and then return to their countries. Joseph also said that they were planning to leave soon to visit some friends to the South.

Liu Xiang scratched his head, stroked his beard and rubbed his nose. There was something special about this baby but why was he born here, in this poor little village? What could he possibly be destined for?

Maria had said that the baby's name was Yeshua, because he would save his people from their sins. Joseph had said he was also called Immanuel meaning God with us. Liu Xiang puzzled over this prophecy. The travelers all talked about what they thought it meant. They set up their beds outside the house. It was a clear and balmy late spring evening. The travelers slept under the stars.

They talked about how strange it was. How they didn't quite know what to do now but how they felt they had met someone important. All of them had questions as to whether this child was really special or not. And as they fell asleep their doubts were about to be answered.

A Shining One stood in their midst.

They clutched their hearts. This being was brighter than the sun. They couldn't stare directly at him … her … it?

"Listen! Return to your own countries by a different route. Herod doesn't want to worship the baby, he wants to kill him. Leave tomorrow."

Philo was excited. He felt like this is what he had been waiting for his whole life. He would travel with the family and be their bodyguard.

Everyone went back to their beds to get a few more hours sleep. Bing couldn't fall asleep. He was thinking too much. He got up because he needed to empty his bladder. He walked faraway enough from the group and found a tree.

As he walked back from the tree he looked up at the stars. A Shining One appeared in front of him. He didn't know if it was the one from before. Bing knelt on the ground with his hands in front of his face.

"What do you want?" asked Bing trembling.

"You are to stay here tomorrow and stop Herod's men from following the family."

"By myself?"

"Others will stay with you. You must remain and make sure that the soldiers do not go down the Southern road. The family need two days to get to safety."

Bing nodded.

"You will see terrible things that the King will do," said the Shining One.

"I have seen terrible things that Kings do. Kings forget justice. Why doesn't God do something? Why doesn't he destroy evil?" Bing pleaded.

"If he destroyed evil now, then no one could stand."

"But why should this child survive and all the other children die?

"You must protect the child."

Bing tried to process all that he was hearing.

"God wants us to kill for him?" Bing asked.

"No," the Shining one said, "He requests that you die for him."

"But why?" Bing asked.

"So that one day, he can die for you."

CHAPTER SIXTEEN

Everyone waved as the family set off on their journey. Philo went with them. He said that the Shining One had told him to protect the family.

Bing sat down. Liu Xiang, Carissa and Arrow asked him what he was doing. Wasn't he leaving too?

"No," said Bing. "The Shining One told me to stay right here and stop the soldiers who are coming to kill the child."

"But that's dangerous," said Carissa.

"We faced many dangers on our journey here and nothing could stop us. I think I'll be fine," said Bing. But he remembered the conversation that he had had with the Shining One.

Bing hugged Arrow.

"You are so brave. I am not worthy to even stand near you. My guilt and shame hang constantly around my neck."

"It's ok Arrow. I forgive you. You go now and help Liu Xiang return to China."

"I'm staying too," said Carissa.

Arrow turned and looked at Carissa. "No," he said. "You must help me escort Liu Xiang back to China."

"No. I'm staying to fight with Bing," said Carissa.

"Where's this coming from?" asked Arrow. "We had plans."

"You'll be OK Arrow."

"But ..." Arrow clenched his teeth. Everyone walked away from Carissa and Arrow to give them some room.

"I know. But this is bigger than us," said Carissa.

"You've gone mad. You don't need to do this. You're innocent. You don't need to sacrifice yourself for anyone."

"I'm not innocent."

"You haven't done anything wrong in your life."

"You wouldn't know," said Carissa.

Arrow looked at Carissa. She was stubborn. He knew he couldn't change her mind but he tried anyway.

"Please come with us along the Southern trade routes. We need you."

"You don't need me Arrow," said Carissa.

"Then I'm staying too," said Arrow.

"No," said Carissa. Liu Xiang is returning home and he needs you."

Arrow looked at Liu Xiang and Liu Xiang nodded. Arrow gritted his teeth and made a huffing noise. He went to his horse and took out his crossbow. The one that could load four bolts at once. He handed it to Carissa and looked her in the eye.

Carissa took the crossbow and slung it over her shoulder. She looked up at Arrow. Bing sat on the ground watching them. He felt for them.

Arrow turned, got on his horse and rode away from the group. He waited for Liu Xiang and the others, he couldn't look back at Bing or Carissa. He had said his goodbyes.

Jacob too said he would stay. He hadn't received any other message from the Shining one, but he was staying. He now believed. He wasn't quite sure exactly what he believed but he knew the child was important.

Bing stood up to say farewell to Liu Xiang.

"Thank you." said Liu Xiang.

"This didn't turn out as you expected, did it?" said Bing.

"It never does," said Liu Xiang.

"Take this," said Bing handing Bao's walking stick to Liu Xiang.

"I understand," said Liu Xiang and he wiped a tear from his cheek. He bowed to Bing and Bing bowed back.

Liu Xiang joined the others and rode out of Bethlehem. Bing, Jacob and Carissa sat and waited for Herod's men to arrive.

They waited a whole day and night camped out at the well. They talked of home and family. Bing tried one more time to convince Carissa to follow after Arrow. She would have none of it.

Bing had set up Liu Xiang's gong near the well. When he heard the sound of Herod's horses in the distance he struck the gong.

The horses headed in the direction of the loud ringing as it echoed over the Judean hills. The head guard rode up to Bing and Jacob.

"Where is the child that you visited? Did not Herod tell you to return to him to tell him about the child? Herod is on his way here now."

"The child is no longer here. Return to your palace."

"Fools. The family will not be able to hide in any of the towns around here. Get out of our way!"

"No."

"Spread out and search for the baby! If we do not find him, we will kill all the babies."

Some of the soldiers tried to ride past Bing, Jacob and Carissa. Jacob swung a rope and it wrapped around two of the riders pulling them off their horses.

Others tried to ride to the side. Bing jumped on a wall and leapt towards the riders, kicking them and knocking them to the ground. Other riders again tried to get past.

Bing ran at them and jumping in the air drew his sword and slashed at the soldiers. They blocked and their horses reared up and backed into the guards behind them.

The head guard got down from his horse. He was a head taller than the other soldiers. He walked forward and drew a large sword, the metal was dark grey with intricate patterns inscribed on the blade.

Carissa swung her sword and the head guard brought his blade up. Carissa's sword shattered. Jacob attacked, swinging his sword with the same outcome. Bing too, swung his sword and although it did not shatter, his blade broke in two. The head guard sheathed his sword and got back on his horse. He sneered and asked, "Do you surrender?"

Bing's heart ached. He knew he could not save the babies. He could save only one. He shook his head, took a breath and held back his tears. He channeled the pain in his heart into his muscles, he surged with energy.

Bing dropped his broken sword on the ground. He picked up a plank of wood, a crossbeam, that was on the side of the road. Splinters from the wood cut into his hands. It focused him on the task.

Carissa picked up a threshing stick. Jacob picked up a gardening fork.

The head guard smiled and said, "Fine. We will deal with you first. It won't take long."

The general gave the orders for the others to charge. Four riders on horseback rode forward.

Bing's plank swirled through the air and hit one soldier on the head. He swung it at another soldier who tried to knock the plank away with his sword but Bing kept swinging the plank and the soldier lunged too hard and not hitting anything, overbalanced and fell off the horse.

Bing grabbed the leg of another man as he dodged his sword and pulled the man off his horse. He grabbed another man, swinging him around. Bing let him go and he flew towards the gong. The loud clang of the gong unsettled the horses and some of them stepped sideways knocking their riders into walls and trees.

Bing jumped onto one of the horses and rode around the soldiers, herding them like cattle. He looked across at Jacob who was swinging his gardening fork in the air. Carissa too was doing a good job of keeping the soldiers busy. The head guard was yelling orders at his men, calling for reinforcements.

Jacob threw the gardening fork at the head guard, knocking him off his horse. Jacob slid under a horse and picked up the head guard and threw him onto the hay.

Bing saw more soldiers arrive at the end of the road. He rode towards them and as he drew close he jumped off his horse. The horses were scared, they whined and stood up on their hind legs, which was unusual for the well trained Roman horses.

Bing's hair stood up on the back of his neck. A shiver ran down his back. He felt like there were other beings fighting around them as well. Unseen beings, some on his side, others not. But this he could not tell. He focused on the here and now. He had to hold off the Roman soldiers for as long as possible. That was their mission.

Jacob was sitting on the head guard and had him in a headlock. "Come closer and I will kill him," Jacob said smiling.

Bing looked back and saw that riders were heading towards the Southern road.

"Come on. We have to stop them." He jumped on a horse and grabbed Jacob's hands pulling him up onto the horse. Carissa, picked up the gong and hurled it back at the riders. It slammed into one of them. She then jumped on a horse too. She caught up with Bing and Jacob racing towards the soldiers heading South. The soldiers disappeared around a hill.

As Bing and Jacob neared the hill they saw that the Roman soldiers had stopped. They were being attacked by Philo.

"What are you doing?" asked Jacob.

"I was disobeying the Shining One when I went with the family." Philo punched one soldier and then another, knocking them out. "My real orders were to stay and fight," said Philo sheepishly. "I really, really wanted to go with the family and be their bodyguard. Then I realized I couldn't live with myself if I was pretending and ..." Another soldier ran at Philo. Philo grabbed the helmet off the soldier's head then head butted him.

"Stop!" Herod had arrived. He was yelling from inside his carriage. "Stop! Who is giving you your orders? Answer me!" yelled Herod.

"I'll tell you. We are getting our orders from the King," said Carissa and she charged with the three men towards the soldiers, pushing the horses back up onto the hill.

Herod ducked back in his carriage and demanded that the driver take him away. "Capture them and crucify them all," yelled Herod. Philo, Jacob and Carissa wanted to chase him but they were unable to. There were too many soldiers blocking the path.

"Let him go," said Bing, "Our job is to not let anyone past this point."

Bing, Carissa, Jacob and Philo stood their ground. They kept up their attack on the soldiers, battering and beating them. The soldiers had the upper hand being on the high ground but for now it did not make a difference. Whenever a soldier on horseback advanced, they were stopped.

Bing, Carissa, Jacob, and Philo fought and fought and fought. The Sun reached its zenith and then started its descent. The four defenders kept fighting. The soldiers were surprised that they were putting up such a fight. Wave after wave of soldiers attacked and tried to break past but they were stopped, injured, forced back.

At one point the soldiers retreated. Bing, Carissa, Jacob

and Philo could breathe. Maybe that was it. Maybe the soldiers wouldn't keep attacking them.

A trumpet sounded. It was a call for the soldiers to regroup. Fresh soldiers had arrived. They attacked the four but even still they could not contain them. The four were able to hold their ground. It would have been much easier to just kill them with arrows or spears, but the Romans wanted to crucify them.

When Bing saw the sun sink to just above the hills, he knew that they could now start to ease off. They kept fighting but slowly, slowly they succumbed to their exhaustion and to the much greater numbers of their opponents. The four were beaten down.

Bing was held up by one of the Roman Soldiers. Two others pinned his arms. Another walked up with a large sword.

"Enough. You've caused us enough trouble." The soldier stabbed Bing through the ribs.

Another soldier beat Jacob with a club. His face was a mess of blood and bone. He sunk to his knees. He was stabbed in the stomach, again and again.

Philo was pinned by four soldiers. He was hacked with swords. Carissa too was hacked but the soldiers backed away when she pulled out the crossbow and waved it around. She shot a bolt through one of the soldier's jaws. "Get away from us. You can leave now," she said as she lay on the ground, propping herself up with her elbow. Philo, Jacob and Bing lay next to her. Wary of the crossbow, none of the soldiers wanted to approach them.

The four could fight no more. On the hill, they lay under a tree. They had held off the soldiers for as long as they could. Under the shadow of the tree on that hill they rested. These were rebels that the Romans would not have the pleasure of crucifying. These were the people that the dragon could kill, but not defeat. They had accomplished their mission.

Bing looked around as the sun sunk behind the hill. They had been fighting all day. It seemed like only moments ago the sun had been rising.

The soldiers left them to go and search the surrounding towns. They disappeared into the growing darkness.

The stars started to twinkle. Bing did not feel the pain of cut flesh or of broken bones, his heart ached for his family and the children who were to be murdered. He tried to push thoughts of them out of his mind. Why was there such evil in the hearts of people? The moon, a new moon looked fresh in the sky. It looked frail but full of hope. Bing cried and his tears mixed with the blood on his face. He looked at the stars and felt small. He closed his eyes.

ABOUT THE AUTHOR

Hi. I hope you enjoyed the story.
I'm an English teacher and an author and I like learning languages. I grew up in Sydney, Australia. My family and I love to live and travel in Asia. I am an avid fan of the greatest international sport: Ping Pong.

You can find out other information about me and my other books at www.michaelbayliss.com or www.facebook.com/michaelbaylissauthor.
If you just want to like the book and not me then go to www.facebook.com/JourneyFromTheEast.

If you have any questions about the historical parts of this book then I would encourage you to seek answers.
Seek and you will find.

Thanks again for reading.
Mikey
@mikey_the_twit

Pronouncing Chinese

A system called Pinyin is used to represent Mandarin. Mandarin is the Chinese language spoken by the majority of Chinese speakers today.

Pinyin looks like the English alphabet and often the sounds are similar. However, there are some different sounds that do not correspond to the English alphabet. The names from the book that are pronounced differently are presented below and a rough pronunciation guide is given. There is more information on the web about how to pronounce pinyin. Visit www.michaelbayliss.com to continue the discussion.

Xiao Zhou - Shi-ow Joe. Pronounce the Shi and ow quickly so it sounds like one syllable. The Shi is pronounced with the tongue behind the lower teeth sometimes written like Hsyi)

(Mrs) **Qian** - Chee-an. Once again say it so it sounds like one syllable. And the Chee (Qi) like the Shee (Xi) is pronounced with the tongue behind the lower front teeth.

(Emperor) **Ai** - Eye (Like eyes on your face)

Liu Xiang - Lee - Ew. Say it quickly so it sounds like one syllable. Shee-ang. Once again say it quickly so it sounds like one syllable and the tongue for the Shee (Xi) is behind the lower front teeth.

Jiaohe - Jow - Her

Xiongnu - Shee-ong. Said as one syllable. Then Nu.

Kashi - Car Sh (The Sh is like the shushing sound but with the mouth in the position when pronouncing the sound i like in it.)

WeiQi - Way Chee

Made in the USA
Charleston, SC
26 October 2014